Emer O'Sullivan, * 1957, aufgewachsen in Dublin, hat dort und in Berlin Germanistik und Anglistik studiert. Sie war Stipendiatin für Kinder- und Jugendliteratur der Berliner Stiftung Preußische Seehandlung und arbeitet jetzt am Institut für Jugendbuchforschung der Johann Wolfgang-Goethe Universität in Frankfurt a. M.
Dietmar Rösler, * 1951, aufgewachsen in Emden, Studium in Berlin. Arbeitet als Dozent im Department of German des King's College der University of London. Schwerpunkte: Sprachwissenschaft, Deutsch als Fremdsprache.
Von den Autoren liegen außerdem vor: «I like you – und du?», «It could be worse – oder?», «Mensch, be careful!», «Butler, Graf & Friends: Nur ein Spiel?», «Butler, Graf & Friends: Umwege» (Bände 323, 374, 417, 531, 647).

Emer O'Sullivan / Dietmar Rösler

Butler & Graf

Ein deutsch-englischer Krimi

Rowohlt

rororo rotfuchs
Herausgegeben von Ute Blaich und Renate Boldt

34.–37. Tausend September 1993

Originalausgabe
Veröffentlicht im Rowohlt Taschenbuch Verlag GmbH,
Reinbek bei Hamburg, Oktober 1988

Umschlagfoto Per Koopmann
rotfuchs-comic Jan P. Schniebel

Gesetzt aus der Garamond (Linotron 202)
Gesamtherstellung Clausen & Bosse, Leck
Printed in Germany
690-ISBN 3 499 20480 0

Inhalt

Erstes Kapitel

in dem Florian einen komischen Anruf beantwortet and in which Maddy suffers a heavy loss

«Whether what?» Verdammt, dachte Florian, warum ist keiner von den anderen ans Telefon gegangen. «Whether a... who...? Madelene Butler? Yes, she lives here. Just a moment.»

Er legte den Hörer auf den Tisch und ging in den Flur. «Maddy», rief er nach oben. Keine Antwort. Mist, gerade war sie doch noch dagewesen. «Maddy?» Typisch, wenn man die Leute mal braucht, sind sie nie da. «Maddy!!!»

Also zurück zum Telefon. Telefonieren auf englisch, der reinste Horror. Und dann noch mit jemandem, der so 'nen schrägen Slang hat. Er nahm den Hörer wieder auf.

«Hallo», sagte er, «she isn't here. Can I take a message?»

Ein Wortschwall vom anderen Ende der Leitung. «You are what? ... Can you speak slowly please... marketing, I see. Yes, of course I know what that is. For British Airways...?»

Er drückte den Hörer mit der Schulter ans Ohr und versuchte, einen Kuli und ein Stück Papier von Mr. Butlers Schreibtisch zu angeln.

«Whether what? Can you say that again? Whether she has been on a plane to Edinburgh lately? Yes, she came back yesterday. Whether she has a computer?»

Eigenartige Fragen, dachte Florian, was zum Teufel ging die das an.

«Why do you want to know?» fragte er zurück. «Oh, I see. Well, yes, she has a computer and no, I don't know whether she brought disks with her to Edinburgh.»

Er hörte jemanden die Haustür öffnen. «Maddy?» rief er.

«Yes?»

«Hold on a minute», sagte er ins Telefon, «Maddy is here now, you can talk to her yourself.»

Maddy came into the room.

«Phone for you», sagte er kurz.

She picked up the receiver. «Hello? Hello?» No reply. «They've hung up», she said to Florian, «who were they and what did they want?»

Florian holte tief Luft. Er dachte an die blöden Übungen, die der Schwatske immer mit ihnen gemacht hatte: er hatte irgendwas auf dem Kassettenrecorder vorgespielt, und sie mußten es hinterher auf englisch zusammenfassen. Ödes Zeug. Der würde sich freuen, wenn er ihn jetzt sehen könnte. Er hörte ihn sagen ‹Siehst du, Florian, das Leben stellt genau dieselben Aufgaben in der fremden Sprache wie ich im Klassenzimmer. Wenn du bloß besser aufgepaßt hättest...› Dieser Armleuchter.

«It was a woman from British Airways Marketing», fing Florian an. «She said they were developing a special small box for people who want to take computer disks with them on the plane. It means you can put them through the security check in the airport without...», er suchte nach dem Wort, «...without all the information disappearing.»

«Being wiped out by the magnetic fields in the x-ray machine, you mean», added Maddy.

Ja, ja, Klugscheißerin, auf deutsch kenn ich auch die richtigen Wörter, grummelte Florian in sich hinein.

«Sounds pretty strange to me», Maddy continued, «are you sure you understood her properly?»

Florian wollte gerade mit einer beleidigten Erklärung loslegen – auf englisch mußte er sich die Einzelteile immer erst im

Kopf zurechtlegen –, da hatte Maddy sich schon umgedreht und war aus dem Raum gegangen.

Wütend ging er auf sein Zimmerchen und warf sich auf das Bett. Um sich treten könnte er bei dem Gedanken, daß die Kurze mit ihrem Alten und seiner Hochseejacht in See gestochen war, daß sogar Sabrina und Klecks jetzt mit ihrem Vater im Mittelmeer dümpelten, daß Konny im Grand Canyon durchs wilde Wasser fuhr und die Pralinen-Zwillinge im Flugzeug mit ihren Eltern auf dem Weg nach Pakistan waren. Wenn er ehrlich war, reizte ihn das eigentlich nicht so. Obwohl Himalaya… – egal, auch das wäre um Klassen besser gewesen, als hier in London den Sommer lang in einer Sprachschule mit Familienanschluß zu versauern, bloß weil der Schwatske seiner Mutter eingeredet hatte, er würde den Leistungskurs Englisch nicht packen, wenn nicht drastische Maßnahmen ergriffen würden. Dieser Blödmann! Null Ahnung. Natürlich konnte er Englisch. Hatte er ja gerade am Telefon bewiesen, selbst das unmögliche Englisch von dieser Frau hatte er kapiert. Aber nein, seine Mutter meinte, Sprachferien müßten sein. Selbst sein letztes Angebot – Nachhilfestunden nehmen – hatte sie abgelehnt. Und nun hockte er in der Wohnung von den Butlers, mit 'ner Tussi, die nur auf Computer zu stehen schien und jeden zweiten Abend Judo trainierte. Florian blätterte mißmutig im ‹Kicker›, den er am Kiosk entdeckt hatte. Aber echte Begeisterung kam nicht auf. Ohne Bundesliga ist eine Sportzeitung eben nur die Hälfte wert.

«How did the people from that British Airways Marketing place get my name and telephone number? And why did they think that I might be interested in a box for disks?» asked Maddy the next morning at breakfast between mouthfulls of muesli with joghurt.

Florian drückte sich gerade leicht gequält das Sägemehl

rein, das unter der irreführenden Bezeichnung ‹sausage› verkauft wurde.

«A growing lad like you should start the day with a proper breakfast», hatte Mrs. Butler gleich am ersten Morgen gesagt, «bacon, eggs, sausages, tomatoes and a few slices of fried bread. That will put hairs an your chest!» Sie lachte zwar dabei, aber meinte es doch wohl ernst. Und so wurde er jeden Morgen gemästet, bevor er zur Sprachschule ging.

Maddy continued, «I mean, how do they know that I have a computer or even that I might have taken disks with me on a flight? It's a bit odd, don't you think?»

Florian überlegte einen Moment. «Another thing», sagte er, «they asked whether you had been on a plane to Edinburgh lately.» Erst jetzt fiel ihm auf, daß das komisch klang. Eigentlich durften doch Fluggesellschaften mit solchen Informationen nicht rausrücken. Aber vielleicht war es ja bei ihrer eignen Marketingabteilung erlaubt. «Yes, it is very odd», beendete er seine Überlegungen.

Maddy had just finished her breakfast and was on her way out of the room when her mother came in.

«I hope you are not off to play with your computer again, Maddy», she said, «I keep telling you it's not good for you. There was something on the radio just now about a computer detective who was killed in Scotland. What is the world coming to!»

Florian war sich nicht sicher, ob sich das auf die Nachricht aus dem Radio bezog oder darauf, daß Mädchen wie Maddy nichts mit Computern zu tun haben sollten.

Maddy sighed. «Yes, Mum», she said, «and it will ruin my eyes as well and then I'll have to wear glasses. And as Uncle Frank always says ‹Boys don't make passes at girls who wear glasses›. Come on, give it a rest Mum.» She left the room.

Fernsehen dient der Entspannung. In Berlin konnte Florian nach der Schule stundenlang vor der Glotze hängen und zwischen allen Kanälen hin- und herschalten. *Zapping* nannten er und die Kurze das, ein englisches Wort, das dieser Schwatske mal wieder nicht kannte. Typisch! Ein irrer Spaß, drei Sendungen gleichzeitig verfolgen zu können. Daß einige der Kabel-Kanäle englisch sendeten, störte ihn dabei nicht. Hier in London, zurück nach sechs Stunden harter Arbeit in der Sprachschule, wollte dasselbe feeling nicht aufkommen, irgendwie störte es total, daß die auf allen Kanälen englisch quatschten. Ob es hier irgendwo deutsche Videos...?

«AAAAAAAAAGH!»

Ein wütender Schrei unterbrach seine Überlegungen. Maddy, who had come home only a few minutes beforehand, burst into the sitting room. «I'll fucking kill you! What have you done to my computer, you...»

Florian war geschockt. «I didn't...» stammelte er.

«Keep your bloody Kraut fingers to yourself. Stupid berk, you've ruined everything. How dare you mess around with my computer!»

Die ist wohl von allen guten Geistern verlassen, dachte Florian. Auch er war gerade erst nach Hause gekommen und war ihrer blöden Kiste garantiert nicht zu nahe getreten. Er hatte überhaupt noch nie in seinem Leben einen Computer angefaßt. Und jetzt diese Furie! «What?» brachte er nur heraus, völlig perplex. Und trotz der Ausspracheübungen am Vormittag kam es als *vot* heraus.

«You've wiped out everything – all my programs, my data, my games, everything. It's just unbelievable. If you really are such a stupid thick German, you should bloody well keep your paws to yourself and leave my things alone. Do you have any idea how much...»

Florian hatte sich wieder gefangen. «Schnauze», brüllte er, «ich war nicht an deinem Scheißkasten.»

«Well, who was it then?» Maddy screamed back at him.

Er mußte wohl sehr belämmert ausgesehen haben, als er merkte, daß Maddy sein Deutsch verstand, denn trotz ihres Zorns mußte sie lachen.

«I haven't been doing O-Level German in school completely for nothing, you know.»

«Tell me what happened», sagte er.

Maddy sat down on the arm of a chair. «When I got home a few minutes ago, I went into my room and found the computer switched on. On the screen it said that it had finished formatting the hard disk and asked if there was anything more to be formatted.»

Florian verstand kein Wort. Maddy tried to explain: «If you format a disk – a floppy disk or a hard disk – you wipe out everything that was on it beforehand in order to prepare it for something new. My hard disk has been formatted, so it means that everything I had in the computer is completely gone.» She looked a bit confused and totally depressed. «You are positive you didn't go near it?» she checked with Florian once again just to make sure.

«I told you I didn't.»

«Then I just don't understand what could have happened. Mum and Dad left the house early this morning, the two of us left later and locked the door after we went. So no one was here until you came home, and you say you didn't go near the computer.»

Florian überlegte, was er sagen konnte, ohne zu zeigen, daß er überhaupt nicht kapierte, was genau mit dem Computer los war oder wie es hätte passieren können.

«Maybe it was a power, äh, a power failure.»

«A power cut, you mean? No, if there had been one it

wouldn't have made any difference – the thing wasn't switched on. Even if it had been, a power cut still can't affect the things which are stored on the hard disk.»

Florian zuckte mit den Schultern. Das sagte ihm gar nichts, und das lag nicht daran, daß sie es auf englisch sagte.

«Anyway», Maddy continued, «the message on the screen about the formatting means that someone must have given the command to format the disk. But who could have done that? If it wasn't such an absurd idea, I would suspect that someone had broken into the house to do it.»

Ein Einbrecher, der nichts klaut, dachte Florian, die spinnt. Laut sagte er: «There wasn't a break-in, there was nothing wrong with the door when I came home.»

«Cheer up», sagte Florian, nachdem Maddy einige Zeit wütend durchs Zimmer gelaufen war und dabei abwechselnd irgendwelche unverständlichen technischen Erklärungen vor sich hin gemurmelt oder mögliche und unmögliche Einbrecher verdächtigt hatte. «Come on, I'll buy you a Coke.»

«Don't want a Coke.»

«An ice-cream, then», ließ Florian nicht locker.

«I don't like ice-cream.» She paused for a moment.

«I'll tell you what I'd like», she decided, «a shandy.»

«A what?»

«It's a mixture of beer and lemonade. Let's go to a pub.»

«Can you just walk into an pub here? Don't they ask you about your age?» fragte Florian.

«We'll soon see.»

Immerhin wollte sie es nicht bei sich in der Gegend versuchen, sondern schlug vor, zu einer Themse-Kneipe zu fahren. «I'm supposed to be showing you the sights of London anyway», sagte sie dabei. She took a piece of paper. ‹Gone to the pictures with Florian› she wrote. «That'll please Mum and Dad,» she said, «they told me to look after you.»

Chapter Two

in which Maddy thinks that she recognizes somebody und in dem Florian sich fürchterlich langweilt, weil ihm dauernd was von Computern erklärt wird und er dabei nur Bahnhof versteht

«Will they really let us into a pub, I mean, at our age?» fragte Florian noch mal, nachdem sie beim U-Bahnhof Hammersmith ausgestiegen waren und sich durch die Autoschlangen auf den Straßen in Richtung Themse durchschlugen.

«Sometimes they do, sometimes they don't», answered Maddy, «but there are pubs where you can sit or stand outside and there are so many people around drinking glasses of beer that they don't really notice or give a damn.»

Florian fühlte sich leicht unwohl. Was er wohl sagen mußte, wenn die Bedienung kam? *One beer and one shandy?* Oder hieß das hier auch so etwas wie ‹einen Halben›? Er zerbrach sich jedoch völlig umsonst den Kopf.

As soon as they got to the pub, Maddy marched straight up to a fellow in a black leather jacket. «Would you mind getting us two pints of shandy?» she asked him.

Der guckte einen Moment verdutzt, warf Florian einen verächtlichen Blick zu und zischte dann Richtung Theke ab.

«Told you», Maddy was triumphant, «easy as pie.»

«I hope he comes back», knurrte Florian und bemühte sich, cool auszusehen.

«Of course he will.» She was right.

«That'll be two pounds eighty, sweetie», the fellow murmured as he gave them their glasses.

Während Florian noch umständlich nach seinem Portemonnaie griff, hatte Maddy schon drei Pfundstücke aus ihrer Hosentasche hervorgezaubert. «Keep the change, pal», she said with a wink. «Let's go over to that bench there», she pushed Florian towards the far corner of the patio, «those two are just leaving.»

«Thanks for the shandy», sagte Florian, nachdem sie sich in eine der Bänke reingezwängt hatten.

«Won't happen every time, I only have a bit of spare cash at the moment because Grandad gave me some when I was up visiting him in Edinburgh. You know that I was up there yesterday and the day before that for his sixtieth birthday, don't you?»

Florian nickte. «How was it up there?» versuchte er das Gespräch in Gang zu halten.

«Fantastic!» Maddy's eyes lit up. «It was the first time I was ever in a plane and I loved it. Flying is really great. I suppose you've flown lots of times.»

«Na klar, äh, of course.» Florian war froh, daß das Gespräch aufs Fliegen kam. Da war er Experte. «Every year since I was small we've flown to holidays – into holidays? – it doesn't matter. We went to Korfu when I was very young and later to Jamaica. My mother loves the sun.»

«Your parents must be very rich then,» Maddy commented. She frowned as she drank a mouthful of shandy. «The most exotic place we've ever gone to on holiday was Penzance, in Cornwall. Boring.» She drank again. «Anyway, it was Grandad's sixtieth birthday and he said that if I came up to see him it would be the nicest birthday present he could imagine. So he sent me a ticket for the flight to Edinburgh. It was really clear when we took off and we had a great view of London from the sky. It was funny seeing everything that small.»

Florian merkte, wie ihm ihre Schwärmerei auf den Geist

ging. Trotzdem, immer noch besser, als wenn sie über Computer redet, dachte er sich. «What did you give him as a present?» fragte er.

«Well, Grandad is really adventurous for an old man. He took early retirement from his firm a couple of months ago – I think they were going bankrupt or something – and he's decided to start on a completely new hobby for his sixtieth birthday. He's bought himself a computer.»

Das darf doch wohl nicht wahr sein, durchfuhr es Florian, da sind wir schon wieder bei dem Thema. Maddy war nicht zu bremsen.

«Anyway, I thought I'd bring along some of my programs and games for him to use – chess, golf...»

«And did he like them», unterbrach Florian mit deutlicher Langeweile in der Stimme. Er befürchtete, daß sie einen ganzen Katalog von Programmen runterrasseln würde.

«I don't know yet. The computer shop didn't manage to deliver the computer while I was there, so I had to leave the disks with him. He said he'll let me know when it arrives. Before he gets to play them though, he'll have to learn about using the computer – about the operating system and that.»

Florian wußte nicht, was ein *operating system* war, aber er wollte nicht fragen; das würde nur dazu führen, daß er wieder eine Vorlesung von ihr erhalten würde. Er fand Maddy ziemlich nervig. Über vernünftige Sachen schien man mit ihr nicht reden zu können. Nur über Computer – und bestimmt auch über Judo. Aber das interessierte ihn noch weniger.

Eine Weile lang saßen beide schweigend da. Nahmen jeder einen Schluck. Sahen sich um. Eine Frau am Nebentisch schrieb gerade einen Brief. Sie war etwa vierzig Jahre alt und hatte kurzgeschnittenes glattes schwarzes Haar mit ein paar grauen Strähnen. Der Rest des Publikums war weitaus jünger.

«I still can't get over it,» Maddy said finally, «how could all the things on my hard disk have been wiped out?»

«Maybe you pressed the wrong button», versuchte Florian eine Erklärung, obwohl er vermutete, daß sie nicht sehr fachkundig klang.

Maddy looked at him sceptically. «Go on, admit it, you don't really have a clue about computers, do you?»

Nicht nur keine Ahnung, dachte Florian, auch nicht das geringste Interesse. «No», antwortete er, «zero knowledge.»

«Do you want to know anything about them?»

«Why not», rang sich Florian eine Halblüge ab, «Wissen schadet ja nichts, äh... it doesn't...»

«...do any harm, you mean?»

«Yeah», nickte Florian.

«Ok,» Maddy sounded business-like, «computer for beginners, lesson one.»

Und das auch noch auf englisch, dachte Florian. Er nahm noch einen Schluck Shandy und sah, wie Maddy einen Zettel und einen Bleistift aus ihrer Tasche hervorkramte und zu erklären und zu zeichnen anfing.

«The parts first», she began. «Screen», she drew what looked like a mini-TV, «you can't watch ‹Dallas› on it, though.» Underneath that she drew a kind of flat box. «These little slits here are the disk drives», she said as she drew them onto the box. «You need one or two of them. That's where you insert your floppy disks with software – programs, games, information, data and whatever. Are you still with me?»

Florian nickte und nippte am Shandy.

«The best kind of computer is one with a hard disk – like mine, for example», she said proudly, «then you only need one disk drive.»

Disks waren also keine Schallplatten, sondern die viereckigen schwarzen Dinger, die Maddy gerade zeichnete. Er hatte bei seinem Freund Manni in Berlin schon welche gesehen. Manni war zwar auch so ein Computerbesessener, aber wenigstens redete der nicht dauernd davon.

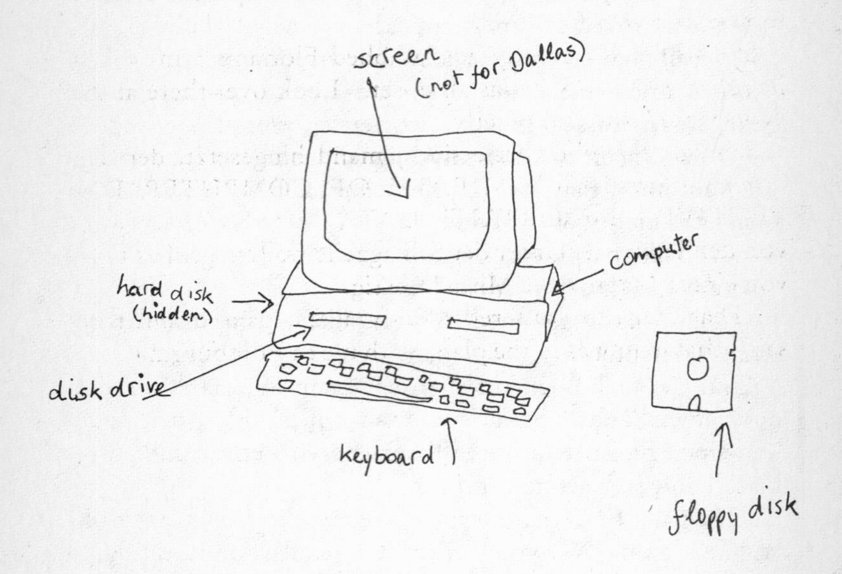

«You see,» Maddy went on, «a floppy disk can store about the same amount of information as you would find in a hundred page book. And the hard disk has several times as much room as a floppy.» Maddy noticed that Florian's thoughts were somewhere else. «This is important for our case,» she added.

Our case? Was für ein Fall, dachte Florian, so'n Quatsch, da hat sie ein paar Daten verlegt oder versteckt oder was auch immer, und schon will sie einen Fall haben.

«Are you listening?» she wanted to know. She continued.

«You can't normally see the hard disk, it's in there.» She drew another arrow which pointed into the box. «And this box here is the acutal computer where all the processing goes on.»

Florian nickte gelangweilt.

«And I suppose I should tell you about the printer and the mouse, but you don't seem...»

She stopped suddenly and grabbed Florian's arm. «That is...that man...» She was all upset. «Look over there at the newspaper,» she said quietly.

Schräg gegenüber hatte sich jemand hingesetzt, der den ‹Evening Standard› las. DEATH OF COMPUTER DETECTIVE – IMPORTANT DATA MISSING, schrie es von der Titelseite. Unter der Schlagzeile war ein großes Foto von einem Mann, etwa Mitte Dreißig.

«That man...» stuttered Maddy again, paused and then said «that man was in the plane with me to Edinburgh.»

Drittes Kapitel

in dem es sich lohnt, Zeitung zu lesen, and in which Maddy's disks are never where they are supposed to be

Nach dieser Entdeckung hatten sie den Pub ziemlich schnell verlassen. Maddy didn't want to talk about it there because she thought she might be overheard, and to tell the whole story in the ‹secret language German›, as she called it, would be too exhausting.

Lauter Spinnereien, dachte Florian; er hatte aber nichts gegen einen Ortswechsel. So hatten sie auf der Hammersmith-Brücke die Themse überquert und spazierten am Ufer entlang in Richtung Innenstadt. Spazierten? Na ja. Je mehr und je schneller Maddy erzählte, desto schneller liefen sie.

Florian entnahm Maddys Wortschwall, daß der Mann auf dem Foto auch im Flugzeug nach Edinburgh gesessen hatte. Er war Maddy deshalb aufgefallen, weil auch er so eine kleine Diskettenbox wie sie in der Hand hatte.

«Do you think the disk boxes could have been verwechselt, äh, confused?» unterbrach Florian sie.

«Swapped, you mean? No. The boxes were identical, both had a smoked-glass part which held the disks and which folded shut into a kind of beige case. Both were big enough to hold about ten disks. But there's no way they could have been swapped. We weren't sitting near each other or anything.»

«Pity», sagte Florian, «that would have made a nice story. *Detective murdered. Important data missing. Little girl's computer wiped out.* And then *Little girl murdered.*»

«Ha ha, very funny.» Maddy was not amused.

Sie waren inzwischen am Wasserreservoir vorbeigekommen. Auf ihrer Seite der Themse sah es grün und ländlich aus. Pärchen lagen am Ufer. Radfahrer überholten sie am laufenden Band, und auf der Themse zogen Ruderboote an ihnen vorbei. Auf der anderen Seite, in Fulham, war das Ufer voller Häuser und Fabriken, nur unterbrochen vom Stadion des Fulhamer Fußballvereins.

«Ok, so you say the boxes can't have been confused, äh, swapped, you had nothing to do with the man, so why are you so shocked by the headline?» wollte Florian wissen. Maddy didn't reply.

Bei ihrer Art des Schnellspazierens kamen die beiden ziemlich bald zur nächsten Themsebrücke, der Putney-Bridge. Die Themse führte Hochwasser und hatte Teile des Putney-Embankments überflutet.

«These people who have stolen your data...» begann Florian.

«Not stolen – destroyed, wiped out, rubbed off, can't you even understand that much?»

Das muß ein ganz schön schlauer Einbrecher gewesen sein, dachte er, einer, der weiß, wie man Daten auf Festplatten löscht. Unsinn, korrigierte er sich, jetzt fange ich schon an, diesen Blödsinn zu glauben. Was war denn wirklich passiert? Wahrscheinlich hatte sie einen falschen Knopf an ihrem Computer gedrückt und alles selbst verloren. Und jetzt verbindet die das mit dem Bild und der Überschrift in der Zeitung, bloß weil sie mit einem schnellen Blick auf das Foto festgestellt hatte, daß der Tote dem Mann im Flugzeug ähnlich sah. Alles Hirngespinste! Da sage noch einer, Computerspiele zerstörten die Phantasie. Ganz im Gegenteil – es scheint sie geradezu anzuregen.

«There is a computer shop down the road from here,» said Maddy. Florian gab sich Mühe, nicht laut aufzustöhnen. «I

have to buy a new transport box for my disks. I left the old one with Grandad.» Sie bogen vom Embankment ab.

«Maybe I was overreacting a bit to my hard disk being wiped clean», said Maddy after they had walked a while in silence. »I suppose it isn't really as bad as all that. I have back-up copies for most of my programs and data on floppy disks and...» She saw by the look on Florian's face that he didn't follow her. «Disk, floppy disk – remember?» she pulled the drawing out of her pocket, «they are the things you keep your data and programs on. And when you have a hard disk on which you store everything, you make back-up or safety copies from time to time. That's in case anything ever happens to the hard disk you don't lose all your data.»

Na also, was soll die ganze Aufregung, dachte Florian, als sie aus dem Computerladen rauskamen und in den Bus nach Hause stiegen, darauf hätte sie ja auch schon früher kommen können.

For the moment Maddy seemed to have forgotten about the break-in. She was busy cursing the traffic jam which was keeping the bus from taking her straight home. She wanted to reload all her programs immediately.

When she opened the front door they heard the telephone ringing.

«You take it,» she shouted to Florian, as she ran up the stairs to her room.

«Hallo», er nahm den Hörer ab. Es war Mrs. Butler.

«Is that you, Florian?» hörte er sie sagen. «How brave of you to answer the phone! I tried to phone earlier but no one was in. Did you go somewhere nice?»

Florian fiel Maddys Zettel mit der Kino-Ausrede ein. «Yeah, we went to the cinema», antwortete er.

«Good», fuhr Mrs. Butler fort, «that is just the thing for

your English. Look, my husband and I both have to work late, so we are going straight from the office to the party.»

Ach ja, beim Frühstück hatte sie gesagt, daß sie und ihr Mann am Abend auf eine Party gehen wollten.

«I'm sorry that we'll be leaving the two of you alone for so long. There's some shephard's pie in the fridge for your tea. Don't stay up too late now! See you in the morning. Bye.»

«Bye.»

Florian wollte gerade die Stufen hinaufgehen, als Maddy heruntergerast kam – völlig bleich.

«It's gone,» she screamed, «the large container with all my floppies in it is gone!»

«You mean there was a second burglar in here while we were away?» Jetzt spinnt sie aber wirklich, dachte Florian und lachte. «Yeah, there's probably a school of burglary around the corner which specializes in computer programs.»

«You idiot!» screamed Maddy who looked like she was going to punch him. «You stupid Kraut, it's not a joke, this is for real. Everything is gone now. All my programs, the games, my data – everything.» She thumped the wall with her fist. «I just don't believe it. Why would somebody wipe out everything on my hard disk and steal all my floppies?»

Nachdem sie sich etwas beruhigt hatte, versuchten sie zu rekapitulieren. Florians Idee von einem zweiten Einbruch war natürlich Unsinn gewesen. Wahrscheinlich hatte Maddy am Nachmittag, als sie die Sache mit der Festplatte entdeckt hatte und sogleich laut schimpfend zu Florian gerannt war, einfach gar nicht bemerkt, daß auch ihre Kiste mit Disketten fehlte.

Wenn die Kiste fehlte, dann sah es vielleicht doch nach einem Einbruch aus, dachte Florian, obwohl ihm die Sache mit der *hard disk* noch immer nicht verdächtig erschien.

«So what do we do now», fragte er, «go to the police?»

«And tell them that there isn't any sign of a burglary but that a container full of disks is missing and that a mystery person has wiped my hard disk clean?»

Florian zuckte mit den Schultern. Klingt nicht sehr glaubwürdig, sagte er sich.

«They wouldn't understand a word anyway, they are probably all computer illiterate,» Maddy continued.

Florian fiel nichts ein. «By the way», sagte er endlich, «the phone – that was your mother. Your parents won't be home till late.»

«That's just great.» Maddy sighed. «Parents! They're never there when you need them.»

«We could buy the newspaper and read about your detective», versuchte Florian sie aufzumuntern.

«Good,» Maddy agreed, «and we can pick up a kebab while we're at it. I'm starving.»

«But there's shephard's pie in the fridge, your mother said.»

«Yuk, I hate shephard's pie. Let's just pick up a kebab and go to the park and eat it there. There's a band playing this evening. And we can read about the detective at the same time.»

Gesagt, getan. Picknick, untergehende Abendsonne, Musik, eine friedliche Stimmung; nur das, was in der Zeitung stand, war nicht ganz so friedlich.

DEATH OF COMPUTER DETECTIVE – IMPORTANT DATA MISSING

Mr. Gordon Mackey (37) died yesterday evening in Leith Hospital, Edinburgh, as a result of injuries sustained in a hit-and-run accident three days ago. Mr. Mackey, a detective, was hit while crossing George St. by a car driving at full speed. The car, a red Volkswagen Passat which had been reported stolen the previous day, was later found abandoned on East Fettes Avenue. The police is continuing investigations.

A representative of Mr. Mackey's detective agency said that he had been «working on a case of computer fraud involving people in high places». He had been working on the case alone. An eyewitness at the scene of the accident claims to have seen a small box of the sort used to transport computer disks in Mr. Mackey's hand. This was thrown up into the air by the impact of the crash, according to the eyewitness. No such box was subsequently found at the scene of the accident. The police would be grateful for any information concerning the container and its contents.

The Local Resident's Association has issued a statement saying how this most recent fatality underlines the need for greater safety measures regarding traffic in the area.

«You see,» Maddy was very excited, «it must have been him on the flight to Edinburgh! What are we going to do?»

Florian suchte gerade im Kopf die Übersetzung von ‹Ist mir doch egal› oder ‹Wieso wir? Hat doch nichts mit mir zu tun›, als eine Stimme seine Sucharbeit unterbrach.

«Hey, Maddy! Long time no see.» Ein Mädchen klopfte Maddy von hinten auf die Schulter.

Maddy turned around. «Sakina! Where have you been hiding. I haven't seen you for ages. By the way, this is Florian – remember I told you my mother arranged to take a German from the language school.»

«Oh yeah. Hi, Florian.»

«Hi.»

Einen Moment lang sagte keiner was, dann unterhielten sich Maddy und Sakina über etwas, was Florian nicht verstand. Er schloß die Augen und dachte an die Postkarte, die er am Morgen erhalten hatte. Sie war von der Kurzen. Aus Madeira. Eine Ansicht vom Silvesterfeuerwerk. Mitten im Sommer. Typisch die Kurze. Viele Grüße stand drauf und ob er denn auch immer brav zur Sprachschule gehe. Und er solle ihr ja schreiben, wie es ihm ergehe. Postlagernd Casablanca.

Maddy and Sakina chatted for a while about this and that.

«By the way, are you doing anything tomorrow?» Sakina asked, «because I was thinking of going out to Wimbledon. I've been following the tennis on the telly all week, whenever I didn't have to do housework, that is, and I'd like to go to see a bit of live action. Are you on?»

Maddy had never been to Wimbledon before and thought it was a great idea.

«We'll have to leave very early to get a place in the queue,» said Sakina. «What about your friend, the dreamer over there,» she nodded towards Florian who was miles away in Madeira, «will we bring him along with us? He looks nice.»

«Well, I've had enough of him for a while,» Maddy said, «I don't want him to come.»

Florian drehte sich auf den Bauch. Was sollte er denn schreiben? Daß er bei einer Familie wohnte, deren Tochter sich für Computer und Judo interessierte, daß sie in einem schmalen Scheibchenhaus wohnten mit einem Garten, der diesen Namen nicht verdiente, so klein war er, daß er jeden Tag in eine Sprachschule ging, fünf Stunden lang die Bank mit einer Schar von blöden Franzosen und Spaniern und einem noch blöderen Typen aus Villingen namens Heinrich drückte, um englische Grammatik zu pauken, und daß es bisher erst einen richtigen Sonnentag gegeben hatte? Das wäre doch ein toller Brief, in dem das alles stünde. Nee, dann lieber gar nicht schreiben.

«Meet you at the railway station at seven o'clock tomorrow morning then, ok?» said Sakina quietly to Maddy as she was leaving the park. «Goodby Florian.» That was much louder.

Florian blinzelte wie einer, der aus dem tiefsten Schlaf geweckt wurde: «Oh, goodbye Sabina.»

«Sakina!»

Als er zu ihr hoch sah, fiel sein Blick auf eine Bank in etwa zwanzig Meter Entfernung. Auf ihr saß ein junges Pärchen und schmuste. Das könnten er und die Kurze sein auf der Jacht, dachte Florian. Trotz dieser Gedanken konzentrierte sich sein Blick auf die Frau, die neben dem Paar saß und Zeitung las. Sie sah der Frau aus der Themse-Kneipe verdammt ähnlich. Fang du nicht auch noch an zu spinnen, ermahnte er sich, es reicht doch, daß die Tussi hier sich alles mögliche einbildet. Trotzdem fragte er Maddy: «Do you see that woman over there on the bench?»

Maddy looked over. «The one with the newspaper?» she asked.

«Yes, do you know her?»

«No, do you?»

«I don't think so, but she does look a bit familiar»

It was getting dark when they left the park to go home. There was no light on in the house. «It's not bad that the parents are at that party. At least we don't have to invent a film we're supposed to have seen,» said Maddy.

Florian lehnte sich gegen die Hauswand, während Maddy nach dem Schlüssel kramte. Dabei stieß seine Hand etwas vom Fenstersims. Mist. Wieso war da ein Blumenkasten?

Maddy bent down. «I don't believe it», she wispered, «I just don't believe it!»

Florian versuchte zu erkennen, worum es sich handelte.

«It's the container with my disks that was stolen. And it looks as if they are all there.»

Chapter Four

in which Maddy and Sakina look at tennis and don't notice much else in Wimbledon, und in dem Florian und Manni zu viel merken und deshalb nicht dazu kommen, sich ein Spiel anzusehen

Casablanca. Sonne. Er und die Kurze an Deck. Die Wellen plätschern leise...

«Florian, Florian, wake up, come on, you're wanted on the telephone.»

Aus der Ferne drang Maddys Stimme zu Florian durch. Wieso war ein Telefon an Bord? Und wieso diese Maddy? Ach ja, die arbeitete ja als Butler an Bord. Sicher servierte sie ihnen gleich einen Shandy.

«Wake up, Florian, come on!»

Langsam dämmerte es ihm. Von wegen Boot und Sonne – London und Sprachschule! Wahrscheinlich einer dieser Kontrollanrufe von seiner Mutter. Ob er auch ordentlich zur Schule gehe. Florian knurrte.

«Come on, get up,» Maddy was getting impatient, «it's someone called Money. Funny names you Germans have.»

Florian blinzelte sie an. «Häh?» Er verstand kein Wort.

«For the last time, you're wanted on the phone. I'm off now. Bye,» she said on her way out.

Florian öffnete ein Auge etwas weiter und schaute auf die Uhr. Knapp sieben. Und so was sollen Ferien sein. Und wieso ging Maddy schon aus dem Haus? Noch ganz verschlafen krabbelte er aus dem Bett und schlurfte in Richtung Telefon.

Maddy ran all the way to the station. On the way she passed by the woman they had seen in the park the evening before. She was just getting into her car.

«I thought you'd never make it,» Sakina said.

«Sorry, but there was a phone call for the German and I had quite a job waking him up.» The train arrived just as they reached the platform.

«Hallo», nölte Florian ins Telefon.

«Hallo, Flo, alter Knabe, hier Manni. Na, wie sieht's aus?»

Florian wurde sofort wacher. «Mensch, Manni! Von wo aus rufst du denn an?» wollte er wissen.

«Aus der Hauptstadt des Königreichs Ihrer Majestät», kam es zurück, «ich bin gestern abend angekommen.»

«Aus London?» Florian konnte es kaum fassen. «Was machst du denn hier?»

«Mein Vater, diese Verkaufskanone, hat von seiner Firma eine Reise nach London und drei Wimbledon-Tickets als Prämie bekommen», fing Manni an zu erklären. Florian war erstaunt. «Super! Und wie lange bleibt ihr? Hoffentlich hast du Zeit, damit wir was zusammen unternehmen können. Ich sterbe nämlich hier vor Langeweile.»

«Was, in Swinging London?» fragte Manni spöttisch. «Das hängt hoffentlich nicht mit der Paukerei zusammen.»

«Klar doch, womit denn sonst?»

«Sag mal, Florian, der Grund warum ich heute so früh anrufe: Wir haben drei Karten für Wimbledon, bloß die arme kleine Irene hat sich doch zwei Tage, bevor wir losfuhren, den Fuß gebrochen und konnte nicht mit. Ist das nicht wahnsinnig traurig?» Manni konnte seine um fünf Jahre jüngere Schwester nicht ausstehen. «Also haben wir eine Karte übrig, und ich dachte, vielleicht hast du Lust...»

«Vielleicht!» platzte Florian dazwischen. «Das wäre doch

phantastisch. Wimbledon! Klar komm ich mit. Wann fahren wir?»

«Die Spiele fangen um zwölf Uhr dreißig an. Wir könnten dich abholen, sagen wir mal...»

«Nein», unterbrach Florian, «ich treffe euch am U-Bahnhof Wimbledon. Eigentlich habe ich von zehn bis vier Schule, und ich will nicht, daß die Leute hier mitkriegen... ok?»

«Ok.»

«Bloody hell, this must be the longest queue I've ever seen. Where does it end?» Maddy and Sakina had just got off the bus at the Wimbledon tennis grounds. Everything had gone well so far; they had changed trains at Clapham Junction and only had to wait five minutes for the one to Wimbledon. The train was pretty full but they managed to get a single seat, which they shared. Outside Wimbledon train station, fleets of double-decker buses waited to ferry the people to the All England Club. It was just after eight o'clock when they got there and thousands of people were queuing back along the road as far as the eye could see. The people were standing on the footpath and kept in line off the road by police barriers.

«You'll see soon enough where it ends because that's where we have to go», said Sakina. They turned their backs on the entrance to the grounds and walked back along the queue on the opposite footpath. «One, two, three, four...» Maddy started to count the steps to their destination.

«You are up early today, Florian», begrüßte ihn Mrs. Butler, als er früher als sonst zum Frühstück kam.

«Yes», antwortete er. Er wollte möglichst schnell aus dem Haus sein, damit die Butlers ihm nicht noch anboten, ihn zur Schule zu bringen.

«Must be in the air today», plauderte Mrs. Butler weiter,

«Maddy went off very early as well and I don't even know where she's gone. Oh well», seufzte sie, «I suppose that's the way it is when children start growing up and doing their own thing.»

O Gott, und so was auf nüchternen Magen. Schnell wechselte Florian das Thema und sagte, daß er vor der Schule noch ein bißchen im Park spazieren und deshalb früher losgehen wollte. Er vertilgte seine Eier, Schinken und Würstchen in Rekordzeit.

«Funny idea», lachte Mrs. Butler, «but the Germans like walking, don't they?»

Die Aussicht auf eine Runde Schule schwänzen und einen Ausflug mit Manni nach Wimbledon hatte Florian in eine aufgeregte, gute Stimmung versetzt. Er fuhr zum Bahnhof Waterloo, kaufte sich eine deutsche Zeitung, setzte sich in das Bahnhofscafé, trank einen Kaffee und begann, gemütlich zu lesen, bis es elf wurde und der Zug nach Wimbledon von Gleis 1 abfuhr.

«One thousand one hundred and ninety three,» proclaimed Maddy when they finally reached the end of the queue. They had followed it all the way up Church Road and on into Wimbledon Park Road, along by the golf course to their right and streets turning off to the left which bore signs saying ‹No waiting in this street 8.30 am – 9 pm› and ‹No queuing in Bathgate Road›. They walked past people lying in sleeping bags who had spend the night waiting there, and others sitting in picnic chairs which they had brought along with them. Some were reading newspapers, a few were tapping their feet and moving their lips to the sound of their walkman, others were chatting to their neighbours. A couple of hundred yards into Wimbledon Park Road the queue seemed to end. But when Maddy and Sakina got there they saw that it had just disappeared into a huge field. There, hundreds of people were waiting their turn to join the queue on the street.

«Oh God,» moaned Maddy, «will we ever make it to the grounds?» Sakina assured her that they would. She had been there a couple of times before, and the queue was always that long. «Never mind,» said Maddy, «I have a story which I can tell you to pass the time while we're waiting. I'll call it ‹The Computer Mystery› and it's a true story.»

«Eh, Mensch, Manni, toll, echt.» Florian umarmte seinen Freund. «Tag, Herr Hutzner. Toll, daß Sie mich mitnehmen. Danke.»

Mannis Vater winkte ein Taxi heran. Ein herrliches großes Londoner Taxi, in dem man sich richtig ausstrecken konnte. «To the tennis, please», sagte Herr Hutzner, «Gate 4.»

«Got proper tickets, then?» antwortete der Taxifahrer, «lucky you.»

Das Taxi fuhr eine Straße mit prächtigen Villen entlang. «Ganz schön anders als die Scheibchenhäuser bei den Butlers», bemerkte Florian. Sie passierten eine schier endlose Schlange von Leuten. «Ej, das ist ja fast wie in Berlin», rief er und wies auf die große Mauer mit Stacheldraht darauf, die das Tennisgelände umgab, «und all die Absperrgitter!»

«Warte, bis du drinnen bist», sagte Herr Hutzner, «dann wirst du sehen, warum alle Leute so von Wimbledon schwärmen.» Das Taxi hielt. «Two pounds forty, please», verlangte der Fahrer. Herr Hutzner gab ihm drei Pfund. «Thanks, gov, hope you have a nice day and no rain.» Florian sah nach oben. Nur einige kleine Wolken waren zu sehen.

«But when I brought the container with the disks to the police last night to have it fingerprinted they just laughed at me,» Maddy continued. «They said there was no crime involved in something which went missing for less than twenty-four hours and then turned up again without any parts missing or damaged. The officer in charge, a funny-looking bald policeman, said that someone must have just been playing a trick on me. And they hadn't a clue what I was saying when I told them about the hard disk.»

«Was Florian with you?» Sakina asked.

«No,» Maddy grunted. «He thinks I'm making it all up.»

«Did the police think he might have hidden the disks then?»

«No, I didn't mention Florian to the police. He's not very important anyway.»

She had come to the end of her story but they hadn't reached the gates yet. They could see them now though, so it would only take another hour or so.

«Wir haben Karten für Court 1», sagte Herr Hutzner, als sie vor einer großen Tafel mit der Überschrift ‹Order of Play› standen. Florian war noch ganz überwältigt. Menschenmassen, und dabei begann das erste Spiel erst in einer Stunde, auf dem Centre Court und Court 1 sogar erst in zweieinhalb Stunden. Und dann die Schlangen draußen.

«Ihr habt eure Karten, nicht?» fragte Herr Hutzner. «Ich werde mich mal ein bißchen im Bewirtungszelt meiner Firma blicken lassen. Seht euch einfach um. Wir treffen uns dann schon irgendwann auf unseren Sitzplätzen, und ich kauf euch Erdbeeren mit Sahne. Die gehören zu Wimbledon. Ok?»

Manni nickte. Er hatte inzwischen entdeckt, daß Steffi Graf ihr Viertelfinale auf Court 3 spielte. «Nichts wie hin», sagte er, «sonst kriegen wir da sicher keinen Platz mehr.»

Maddy and Sakina just made it to the gates as play was about to start. They were very pleased when they got in. Sakina explained to Maddy that there was no point in going to

Court 1 or the Centre Court. There was only room for a few non-ticket holders there, and it would be full already. Instead they thought they'd have a mooch around the outer courts. Flach and Seguso were going to play in the men's doubles on Court 14, so the girls decided they'd start off there.

Eine Stunde vor Spielbeginn auf Court 3 hatten Manni und Florian gerade noch einen Platz ergattert. Das Warten auf den Spielbeginn dauerte länger als das ganze Match, denn Steffi Graf jagte ihre Gegnerin in weniger als einer Stunde mit 6–3, 6–1 vom Platz. «Und jetzt?» fragte Florian, «Court 1?»

«Laß uns noch ein bißchen rumlaufen», meinte Manni, «14 sieht ganz interessant aus, vielleicht können wir uns da noch reindrücken.»

«Da ist der Aufgang zu 14», sagte Manni, als sie dort ankamen, und ging Florian voran.

«Toll... Moment!» Florian stoppte und zog Manni zurück. «Dahinten sitzen Maddy und Sakina. Deswegen ist die also heute früh so geheimnisvoll abgerauscht.»

«Die Kleine da mit dem grünen Pullover und die Inderin?»

«Ja. Komm, die muß ich ja heute nicht gerade treffen. Gehen wir lieber woanders hin.»

«Von mir aus», brummte Manni, «obwohl...» Er hielt inne. «Ich werd verrückt. Da hat gerade einer deiner Lady die Handtasche geklaut.»

«WAAAAS?»

«Ja, der Typ dahinten mit dem blauen Blazer. Komm, hinterher!» Der Mann verließ die Tribüne durch den anderen Aufgang. Manni und Florian drehten um und liefen ihm nach. In dem Gedränge war es gar nicht so einfach, den Mann nicht zu verlieren. Er ging in Richtung Centre Court. In dem

Menschenknäuel vor der *Order of Play*-Anzeigetafel gelang es Manni, recht nahe heranzukommen.

Unter dem Blazer hatte er ein weißes Hemd an. Er trug einen Schlips und war vielleicht so um die dreißig Jahre alt, schätzte Manni. Eigentlich sah er nicht aus wie ein Dieb. Aber wie sehen Diebe schon aus?

«Der hat die Handtasche ja gar nicht», bemerkte Florian enttäuscht, als sie sich durch die Massen vor der Ergebnistafel bei Court 15 drängelten.

«Klar, die hat er sofort an einen Komplizen weitergegeben. Jetzt nur dranbleiben.»

Sie schafften es, den Mann im Auge zu behalten.

«Hoffentlich hat er keine Centre Court Tickets», sagte Manni, als sie nach rechts in Richtung Centre Court abbogen, «da kommen wir mit unseren Tickets nämlich nicht rein.»

«So,» said Maddy during the next break of play, «I've told you all my news, tell me what you've been up to. I hadn't seen you around for ages till yesterday evening.»

Sakina sighed. «That's because I haven't been around,» she admitted. «About three weeks ago I sneaked out to go to a party Brad was having, and my sweet older brother went and told my parents. I could have wrung his neck.»

Maddy nodded sympathetically. She was glad she didn't have an older brother. They caused nothing but trouble.

«It meant I was practically not allowed to leave the house since then,» Sakina continued, «and had to do loads of extra housework as punishment. It wasn't fair.»

«Your parents are very strict, aren't they?» Maddy said.

«They aren't half as bad as most Asian parents,» Sakina stuck up for them, «and they're getting better. By the way,» she added, «you haven't told me all your news. I haven't heard you mention the name Philip once.»

Maddy tried to sound as indifferent als possible. «Oh *him*? He's ancient history.»

The look on her face told Sakina to ask no further questions.

Der Mann ließ den Aufgang zu den Sitzplätzen im Centre Court rechts liegen und marschierte direkt auf die lila-grün-weißen Markisen mit den Aufschriften *Champagne and Pimms* und *Strawberries and Cream* zu.

«Wenn der jetzt zu den Erdbeeren geht, gehst du auch rein, holst dir'n paar, stellst dich möglichst in seine Nähe und winkst mir zu. Dann mache ich ein Foto von euch, und wir haben ihn.» Manni war mit Feuereifer dabei. Florian ging in die Kassenschlange, zahlte seine £ 2.50 und erhielt einen kleinen Becher Erdbeeren mit Sahne.

Sie hatten kaum das Foto geschossen, da verließ der Mann den Stand auch schon wieder und marschierte in Richtung Courts 2 und 3 weiter. Leise fluchend stellte Florian seine noch halbvolle Erdbeerschale ab und eilte hinter Manni und dem Mann her.

«Halt, kannste etwa nicht lesen?» schimpfte Manni ärgerlich. Florian war in die *No Entry*-Passage gelaufen und kämpfte gegen einen Strom entgegenkommender Leute, während der Mann den *One Way* Gang entlang verschwand.

«Mann, das ist ja schlimmer als vor Weihnachten auf der Schloßstraße», stöhnte Florian.

«Hier ist die *Viewing Lane*, da kannste rumstehen und warten, daß deine Helden rauskommen», erklärte Manni im Laufen, «deswegen gibt's hier immer so'n Gedränge, und deswegen haben sie so'n Einbahnsystem aufgebaut.» Manni zog Florian weiter. Wo war der Kerl bloß?

«By the way,» Sakina asked Maddy while the players were resting between games, «did you tell Florian where you were going today or was he asleep when you left?»

«No, I told you, I had to wake him up,» she replied, «some German friend of his phoned.»

Sakina looked at her. «You don't really like him, do you? I thought he looked quite nice.»

Maddy thought for a moment. «Well,» she said, «I don't exactly dislike him, it's just that I don't like him very much. He sticks his nose up at everything – he thinks our house is too small and that the food is awful here. The weather really annoys him, too, and he keeps talking about the wonderful places he's been to. Most of his friends are in really exotic countries on holidays or else cruising around the world in yachts. They all have so much money. I suppose that's what's annoying me.»

«It's not his fault if his parents are rich,» Sakina replied.

«No,» said Maddy, «I suppose not. But he still gets up my nose. And he hasn't a clue about computers. Come on, Flach,» she screamed. He had just served a double-fault.

Sie hatten Glück. Der Mann stand vor dem Stehplatzaufgang zu Court 2 und musterte die Schlange. Vielleicht wollte er raufgehen. Manni blickte zur Anzeigetafel für diesen Court. Connors vs. Kühnen: 5–7, 7–6, 7–6, 6–7, 3–3. Da wäre er jetzt auch gern gewesen. Halb hoffte er, daß der Mann raufging, und er so den fünften Satz sehen konnte.

Florian blickte sich um. Oben, am Ende von Court 1, führte ein Reporter im Fernsehraum ein Interview.

«Ej, weiter», unterbrach Manni seinen Rundblick, «unser verdächtiges Subjekt läuft weiter, hoffentlich nicht zum Ausgang.» Hinter ihnen ein Aufschrei: *Boris, Boris*. «Die Fans sind wieder am Werk», sagte Manni.

Der Mann ging nicht zum Aufgang, sondern um Court 2 herum. *Jimmy! Come on Jimbo!* klang es vom Court.

«Muß'n tolles Spiel sein», kommentierte Manni. «Egal. Weiter. Hinterher.» Der Mann ging hinter den Hecken zwischen den Courts 7 und 11 entlang und bog dann in den Gang zwischen den Courts 11 und 12 ein.

Boris, Boris they heard the screams of the fans. «Now there's a German I wouldn't mind having in my house for the summer.» Maddy sighed. The game they were watching was over.

«Is Florian interested in tennis?» Sakina wanted to know.

«Florian, Florian, can't you talk about anything else?» Maddy was irritated. «Come on, let's go. I'll treat you to a Coke.»

She bent down to pick up her bag. Funny, it wasn't beside her seat. She looked on the floor. It wasn't there either. Her bag was gone. Bloody hell, what should she do?

They looked to see if they could find one of the hundreds of uniformed people who performed various duties in the Wimbledon grounds. An officer of the London Fire Brigade was standing at the exit of the court. He told her where to go. Court 2 west. Lost property office. Maybe someone had handed the bag in.

Der Mann ging in eines der Zelte am Ende des Gangs. *United Chemicals* stand groß drauf. Als Florian und Manni hinterhergehen wollten, wurden sie freundlich, aber bestimmt daran gehindert. «I'm sorry boys, but you have to have a special invitation to go beyond this point», sagte eine junge uniformierte Frau und drückte sie sanft zur Seite, um Platz für eine elegante Frau in Nadelstreifenjacke und -rock zu machen.

«But we...» Florian stockte, «we only want to look.»

«I'm sorry but this area is reserved for the hospitality marquees of the sponsoring firms. They entertain their business friends there. And they don't like anyone else wandering around.»

«Und nu?» fragte Florian.

«Bin ich Prophet?» gab Manni zurück.

«Wir müssen wohl zu den Mädchen und ihnen erzählen, was passiert ist. Immerhin haben wir ein Foto von dem Typen. Aber dann hauen wir wieder ab. Es reicht, wenn ich die sonst dauernd sehe.»

«Die kommen mit ihrem Ticket sowieso nicht auf Court 1», sagte Manni. «Ok, wir gehen dahin, aber laß uns an Court 2 vorbeigehen, vielleicht kriegen wir noch das Ende von Connors gegen Kühnen mit.» Sie gingen zurück.

Als sie bei Court 2 um die Ecke bogen, Maddy and Sakina came out of the lost property office. «Florian! What are you doing here!» und «Gott, da ist die Handtasche ja», shouted Maddy and Florian simultaneously.

Fünftes Kapitel

in dem eine komplizierte Verwechslung entwirrt wird and which ends with a plan of action

Es dauerte eine ganze Zeit, bis alle vier kapierten, was passiert war, vor allem, da am Anfang alle durcheinander in zwei Sprachen redeten. Maddy found it very odd that Florian and his friend should be more surprised to see her handbag than to see her. Besonders Manni konnte es einfach nicht fassen, daß die Handtasche da so einfach von Maddys Schulter baumelte.

After Florian and Manni had told the story of their chase Maddy said: «That's strange. I thought I had just left the bag somewhere or dropped it or something. That's why we went to the lost property office. The man there said I was very lucky, that a woman had just left it in five minutes before I arrived.

«A woman?» fragte Manni überrascht.

«It's nice to know that there are still some decent people left,» said Sakina.

Oder sie war die Partnerin von dem Mann, dachte Florian. Vielleicht sogar die Frau, die sie im Park gesehen hatten. Wenn Leute Disketten klauen und zurückbringen, warum dann nicht auch Handtaschen? Florian ertappte sich dabei, daß er Maddys Theorie von den gestohlenen Disketten vom Vorabend jetzt voll übernommen hatte.

Manni wollte von Maddy wissen, ob irgend etwas fehlte.

«No, nothing at all,» she replied, «that's why I thought I really had lost it. But if you saw someone stealing it... what with that and all the trouble with the disks... it just can't be a coincidence.»

«Trouble with disks?» unterbrach Manni.

Florian stöhnte auf. «Das hätteste lieber nicht fragen sollen, jetzt kannst du dir nämlich die nächste Stunde Tennis abschminken.»

«Wieso?»

«Maddy steckt in einer komischen Geschichte mit Computern drin.»

«Oh, toll!»

Toll? Na ja, Manni war eben auch einer dieser Computer-Freaks. Florian wandte sich den beiden Mädchen zu. «Did you understand that?»

Maddy and Sakina looked at each other. Sakina had done O-Level German with Maddy, but she wasn't as good as her friend in that subject.

«I think so,» Sakina finally said, «except for the bit about the make-up and the hour's tennis. That didn't seem to make sense.»

Manni lachte. «No, *abschminken* is..., well, it means you can forget about it. By the way, I'm Manni. I think Florian has forgotten that gentlemen usually introduce their friends.»

«Und das ist Sakina», Maddy replied, «und ich bin Maddy.»

«Das weiß ich schon», sagte Manni.

«Kennt Sakina schon die Geschichte mit den Disketten?» wandte sich Florian, dem der plötzliche Sprachwechsel nicht ganz geheuer war, an Maddy.

«Yeah, she told me all about it while we were waiting in the queue,» Sakina answered for her. «Do you know about it?» she turned to Manni.

«Know what?» antwortete der.

Florian seufzte. «He doesn't.»

«Ok,» Maddy decided, «let's go to one of the outside courts. They'll be empty by now so we can talk there.»

«Und ich erzähl dir auf dem Weg dahin, was bisher passiert ist», sagte Florian zu Manni. Der sah zur Anzeigetafel von Court 1 und schien hin- und hergerissen. «Na gut, gehen wir», sagte er dann, «mein Alter wird sich wundern, wo wir bleiben.»

Auf dem Weg zu Court 17 berichtete Florian von den Ereignissen der letzten beiden Tage. Was er dabei erstaunlich fand, war, wie ihn Maddy immer wieder unterbrach, um einige Details zu korrigieren oder genauer zu beschreiben. Er wußte gar nicht, daß sie so gut Deutsch konnte.

«Na ja», brachte er die Geschichte zu Ende, «mir kam das alles ein bißchen wie Spinnereien von Maddy vor. Ich meine, das mit der Festplatte hätte gut ein Fehler von ihr gewesen sein können, und wenn eine Kiste mit Disketten verlorengeht und ein paar Stunden später wieder auftaucht und es fehlt gar nichts – das sieht doch nicht automatisch nach etwas Verdächtigem aus, oder? Aber die Sache mit der Handtasche so kurz danach – es sieht nun so aus, als ob da wirklich etwas faul ist.»

Während Manni von Maddy genauere Computer-Details wissen wollte, unterhielten sich Florian und Sakina.

Sakina's German wasn't as good as Maddy's but she could still understand quite a bit. They talked about tennis. «You know that my name is Graf», sagte Florian, «just like Steffi.»

Sakina's eyes lit up. «Are you related to her?»

Florian überlegte, ob er ihr eine Geschichte von seiner Cousine Steffi vorspinnen sollte, aber er hatte wohl zu lange überlegt.

«Of course,» Sakina laughed, «she's your sister, isn't she? Just like Pat Cash is your friend Money's cousin.»

Maddy hatte recht. Court 17 war leer. Die vier setzten sich hin. Maddy summed up what they knew: It was clear that some people wanted something which they thought she had – most likely a floppy disk. But she didn't have whatever it was.

Manni meinte, nach allem, was er gehört habe, könne es sich nur um die Diskette des Detektivs handeln. «Es war kein Unfall. Der Detektiv ist umgebracht worden, die Diskette, die er dabei hatte, war aber offensichtlich nicht die gesuchte, sondern eine andere», löste er den Fall im Handumdrehen. Maddy und der Detektiv mußten irgendwie ihre Diskettenbox vertauscht haben.

Florian and Sakina nodded in agreement. But Maddy remained sceptical.

«How could we have? We weren't even sitting next to each other. I mean, if we had been, they could have got mixed up in the hand-luggage compartment or somewhere. But we weren't.»

«Maybe it didn't happen *on* the plane,» suggested Sakina. «Could they have been swapped before you got on or after you got off?»

«I don't think so,» Maddy said and thought about it.

«Mußtest du irgendwann die Box, äh, sorry I mean, did you...» Manni brachte seinen Satz nicht zu Ende.

«Na klar, die Sicherheitskontrolle», sprang Florian ein, «das Gerät, wo das Handgepäck mit Röntgenstrahlen oder so was gecheckt wird.»

Sakina was lost, so Maddy tried to sum up what the two boys had just said. «Yes,» she then added, «but I didn't put my disk box through that x-ray. The data gets wiped out that way. So I asked the guard to look at it by hand. He took the box and brought it to the other side, to the place where the normal hand-luggage comes out of the machine after it is checked.»

«And what were you doing during that time?» Sakina asked. She had never flown and couldn't really imagine the scene.

«While he did that I was being frisked by a female officer.»

«*Frisked*? Noch nie gehört, was heißt denn das?» wollte Manni wissen. Maddy machte es gleich an ihm vor.

«Aha», er wurde ganz rot dabei, «abgetastet.»

«Well, and afterwards I just picked up my box at the other side where the normal hand-luggage comes out of the x-ray machine,» Maddy continued her description.

«Da hättest du doch zum Beispiel die falschen abholen können», meinte Florian.

«I suppose so», Maddy admitted, «but I didn't see a second box. Nor that detective. He was probably stuck in the queue for men. There were loads of businessmen on the flight, so the male officer had more to do. The men had longer to wait for their frisking. I went straight through.»

«Ej, jawohl, genau, das ist es», rief Manni aufgeregt. Er war plötzlich Feuer und Flamme und sprach sehr schnell. «Also paßt auf: erst kommt der Detektiv an. Er gibt sein Handgepäck in die Maschine und die Diskettenbox dem Kontrolleur. Dann stellt er sich in die Warteschlange für das Abtasten für Männer. Der Kontrolleur kontrolliert die Disketten und stellt sie auf die andere Seite, zum anderen Handgepäck. Jetzt kommst du, Maddy. Du gibst deine Disketten dem Kontrolleur, der überprüft sie per Hand, ist vielleicht noch mit was anderem beschäftigt, du gehst zum Abtasten, schwupps, das geht ganz schnell, keine Schlange, du gehst durch, nimmst die Diskettenbox, die da ist, denkst natürlich, das ist deine, ist aber in Wirklichkeit die vom Detektiv, deine hat der Kontrolleur noch gar nicht rübergestellt, also nimmst deine – eigentlich seine – Diskettenbox, gehst in den Warteraum. Der Kontrolleur hat inzwischen deine Disketten überprüft, legt sie hinten ab, der Detektiv kommt endlich mit dem Abtasten an die Reihe, kommt raus, nimmt ganz natürlich seine – also deine – Diskettenbox und geht in den Warteraum. Ja, so muß es gewesen sein.» Er sah sehr mit sich zufrieden aus.

Sakina and Maddy just stared at him. Maddy thought she had understood the gist of what he had just said. Sakina had understood nothing – except for all the *gehsts*. They went through it all again, this time pretending they each were someone in the scene at the airport. When they acted it out that way, they could get a clearer picture of what Manni had suggested.

«Oh yes,» Sakina exclaimed, «it really could have happened that way!»

«*Could*,» Maddy emphazised, «but not necessarily *did*.»

«So,» Sakina continued, «when the detective was hit by the car, the gangsters didn't get the disk they were looking for.»

«Und als sie herausgefunden hatten, daß es die falsche war», ergänzte Manni, «haben sie wahrscheinlich aus dem British Airways Computer die Passagierliste geklaut. Deshalb also dieser komische Marketing-Anruf. Die hatten überall angerufen, um herauszufinden, welcher der Passagiere Disketten dabei hatte. Vielleicht bist du auch nicht die einzige, der lauter so komische Sachen passiert sind.»

Sakina butted in again: «That means that the disk they are looking for is in Edinburgh, right? But if it is, then why hasn't your Grandad been in touch with you? He must have found out by now that the disk isn't what you said it was.»

Vielleicht ist er überfallen worden, dachte Florian. Aber das sagte er lieber nicht. «Weißt du seine Telefonnummer auswendig?» fragte er Maddy statt dessen. She nodded. Manni kramte eine *Phonecard* hervor. Normalerweise lachte er immer über seinen Vater, der an jedem fremden Ort sofort Briefmarken, Sammelfahrscheine und Telefonkarten kaufte. Man kann nie wissen, wozu's gut ist, sagte er immer. Nie war's zu was gut, außer daß sie zu Hause eine Schublade mit Marken und Scheinen aus aller Welt hatten. Aber jetzt hatte er immerhin eine Telefonkarte für Ferngespräche.

Maddy left. Fifteen minutes later she was back. «I talked to

Auntie Dorothy, my father's sister. She said that the computer still hadn't arrived and that Grandad had gone off fishing for a week.»

Immerhin ist er nicht überfallen worden, dachte Florian.

«So the disk hasn't been used yet. Anyway, I made up a story that I had copied the wrong program and wanted to correct it before the computer arrived, and asked her if she could send it back to me.»

«Ist das nicht ein bißchen gefährlich», meinte Manni, «sie könnte in der Post verlorengehen oder sonst was.»

«Besonders in der britischen Post», fügte Florian hinzu, «wo die Angestellten offensichtlich mehr Zeit damit verbringen, das Abbild Ihrer Majestät auf den Briefmarken zu bewundern, als die Briefe zu befördern.» Die Karte von der Kurzen hatte immerhin zwölf Tage gebraucht, bevor sie ihn erreichte.

«Ha, ha,» Maddy didn't find that very funny. «Anyway, she's not sending it by post. My cousin Janet is coming down to London for an interview for a job tomorrow. She's arriving at King's Cross at eight minutes past one.»

«Good,» Sakina was pleased, «then we'll finally know what this is all about.»

Florian war sich da nicht so sicher. Erst mal war völlig unklar, was auf der Diskette drauf war und ob sie was mit ihr anfangen konnten, und dann – wenn diese Leute Maddy gefunden und beklaut hatten, würden sie sie nicht auch zum Bahnhof verfolgen?

«You're probably right,» Sakina agreed, «what can we do?»

«Ich hab's», strahlte Florian, «wir drehen einfach den Spieß um.»

«What's a *Spieß*?» asked Madda and Sakina at the same time.

«Six games all. Tie-break», verkündete der Schiedsrichter auf dem Nachbar-Court. Aber keiner der vier schien ein Auge für die Spannung auf dem Tennisplatz zu haben, als Florian seinen Plan entwickelte. Als sie abends aus Wimbledon wegfuhren, machten sie alle einen sehr zufriedenen Eindruck. Und das lag nicht nur daran, daß sie nach all den unvorhergesehenen Störungen noch ein richtig tolles Doppel auf Court 1 gesehen hatten, auf den alle vier schließlich mit Hilfe der zwei Karten von Manni und Florian gekommen waren.

Chapter Six

in which Maddy and Florian are used as bait und in dem Sakina und Manni zur Verfolgung starten

«Hallo, Jasmin, bitte kommen. Jasmin, bitte kommen. Irgend etwas Neues?»

«Hello, Zentrale, hier nichts Neues», quäkte Sakinas Stimme.

Florian schmunzelte. Selbst durch das Walkie-Talkie klang Sakina freundlich, offensichtlich hatte sie es ihm nicht übelgenommen, daß er als Tarnnamen für sie zuerst *Curry* vorgeschlagen hatte. Ganz anders als Maddy. Die hatte er *James* nennen wollen, wie Butler nun mal heißen. Mit einem verächtlichen Blick hatte sie das abgelehnt. Und dann durfte er sich nicht mal *Earl* nennen. So eine Spielverderberin.

«For God's sake stop being so bloody formal with all your code-names and ‹bitte kommen› nonsense,» Maddy said impatiently, «anyway, I'm leaving now.» She felt quite nervous and didn't particularly like the part she had to play in the plan they had worked out. And she liked the code-name they had agreed on – *Köder* – even less, although it was the right term for what she was at the moment – a bait.

Florian war viel zu begeistert, um sich von Maddys Einwänden beeindrucken zu lassen. «Tennis, hörst du mich?»

«Bin ja nicht taub», antwortete Manni.

«Mein Gott, hast du noch nie im Fernsehen gesehen, wie man das ordentlich macht?» schimpfte Florian. «‹Hörst du mich› heißt ‹bist du da›, verstanden?»

He must have enjoyed playing Cops and Robbers when he

was little, thought Maddy. «Look, I'm really leaving now, so maybe you can stop playing games,» she said, «I hope it works.»

Hoffen wir doch alle, dachte Florian. «Köder verläßt die Zentrale. Köder verläßt die Zentrale», informierte er Manni-Tennis, «verstanden? Over.»

«Na klar doch, unter», brummte der zurück.

«Jasmin, hallo, Jasmin, Köder geht los, verstanden?»

«Yes, äh, ja», Sakina answered. She felt uncomfortable sitting on a rather uneven wall of a house near the corner of The High Road. And having to speak German wasn't making her feel any better. But it was a good thing that they had a kind of secret language. And she liked the code-name she had chosen. Jasmin was her favourite scent.

Maddy walked down the street towards The High Road. Don't look around, she thought, just walk naturally. She passed by Manni, who was pretending to repair his bike on the pavement.

«Hallo, Tennis, irgendwas zu sehen?»

Manni antwortete nicht.

«Hallo, Tennis, ej, was ist denn los?» wiederholte Florian.

«Immer ruhig, Zentrale, und bitte die Form wahren, ja? Ich kann doch schlecht mit dir reden, wenn Mad-, äh, Köder hier gerade vorbeiläuft. Nichts Neues. Kein Schwein zu sehen. Over.»

When she got to the computer shop, Maddy bought ten disks and asked for four envelopes suitable for sending them in the post. Sakina and Manni followed her from a distance after she left the shop, to see whether anyone else was watching or following her.

Ab und zu fragte Florian von der ‹Zentrale›, ob sie schon

jemanden gesichtet hatten, aber jedesmal kam als Antwort ‹nein›.

Florian war enttäuscht. Dabei hatte der Plan so vielversprechend geklungen. Es war offensichtlich, daß die Leute hinter der Diskette her waren. Es mußte irgendwas drauf sein, das keiner zu sehen bekommen sollte. Deswegen hatten die auch vorsichtshalber alles, was auf der Festplatte war, gelöscht, falls Maddy die gesuchte Diskette darauf kopiert hatte. Soviel hatte nun sogar er begriffen. Dann hatten sie alle Disketten, die Maddy hatte, erstmal mitgenommen, um sie zu kontrollieren. Natürlich fanden sie nicht, was sie suchten. Um möglichst wenig Aufmerksamkeit zu erregen, brachten sie die Disketten wieder zurück. Ganz schön schlau. Obwohl sie bisher nicht das gefunden hatten, wonach sie suchten, mußten sie aber immer noch glauben, daß Maddy es hatte – ansonsten wäre die Episode mit der Handtasche nicht gewesen. Bloß auch da hatten sie kein Glück – in der Tasche war die Diskette nicht. Also suchten sie noch...

«Köder geht zur Zentrale», unterbrach Sakina-Jasmin Florians Gedankengang, «what will I do, sorry äh... I mean – oh, to hell with German. Over.»

«Bleib, wo du bist», antwortete Florian. Dasselbe sagte er auch Manni.

«Well, did they see anyone?» asked Maddy anxiously when she got back home, or to the ‹Zentrale› as Florian would prefer her to call it. Er schüttelte den Kopf.

«Blast it!» she cursed. «What do we do now?»

«We'll go on as planned», sagte er, «they must turn up sometime. In the worst case I will have to come back and we will start again. I won't post the disks until we know that someone is seeing me.»

«Watching you, you mean», she corrected him automatically.

Während Maddy die neuen Disketten formatierte und auf jede ein Spiel kopierte, überprüfte Florian in Gedanken noch einmal, ob sie auch keinen Denkfehler gemacht hatten.

Wenn diese Leute die Diskette wollten und wenn sie meinten, daß Maddy sie hatte, dann mußten sie an ihr dranbleiben. Deshalb hatten Manni und Sakina draußen Posten bezogen, um herauszufinden, wer Maddy beobachtete, wer die Verfolger waren und wo sie hingingen. Gleichzeitig mußten sie von Maddy abgelenkt werden, damit die um eins unbeobachtet ihre Cousine und die echte Diskette abholen konnte. Deswegen hatte Maddy auffällig Disketten und Versandtaschen einkaufen sollen, und in ein paar Minuten würde er genauso auffällig mit diesen Versandtaschen zur Post gehen, die Verfolger hoffentlich hinter *ihm* her. Sakina und Maddy waren vom letzten Teil des Plans nicht so überzeugt gewesen.

«Do you really think they'll believe that Maddy would keep the disk, copy it and send it away instead of going straight to the police with it?» hatte Sakina gefragt. «Don't you think they must know by now that Maddy doesn't actually have it but are hoping that she might lead them to it?»

Aber ob die Leute das mit dem Versand glaubten oder nicht, so hatten sie schließlich entschieden, war egal; wichtig war nur herauszufinden, wer hinter ihr her war. Und dafür war der Plan auf jeden Fall gut.

«Hello Zentrale», meldete sich Sakina wieder. «Jasmin here. Park is sitting here in a car, a green Fiat Uno.» She stopped. Maybe the woman had a radio or some sort of receiver in her car. It was probably better to stick to the secret language, German, after all.

«Park sitzt in einem Auto. Sie ist gerade erst gekommen, aber das Auto steht schon lange da. Over.»

Na toll, dachte Florian, es klappt ja doch. «Danke, Jasmin. Bleib auf Posten», antwortete er. Er informierte Manni-Tennis über den ersten ‹Besucher›.

Maddy had finished copying and had started to write the addresses. She was sending a disk to Sonja Howard in Penzance, Henk van Woerden in Utrecht and Una Burke in Dublin, three computer pen-friends of hers, and one to Mark Säger, a cousin of Manni's in Berlin.

«I'm ready with these now,» she said to Florian. «So, now it's your turn to be the bait. You go to the post office, post them and then wander around the place. Remember, we agreed that you can go anywhere as long as it isn't near King's Cross. Sakina and Manni will tail whoever might follow you. I'll leave for King's Cross in about an hour to pick up Janet. Till then I'll stay by the phone here – oh excuse me,» she added mockingly, «I mean of course at the *Zentrale*, and wait for Sakina-Jasmin and Manni-Tennis to call. Right?»

Florian nickte. «One more thing», sagte der dann, «my school. Could you phone and say I'm sick. I don't want to schwänz, I mean, not be there two days behind each other.»

«Play truant two days in a row, you mean. Sure, I'll phone and tell them that our poor German has just slipped on a banana skin and won't be able to come in today. Or even better,» she added, «I'll tell them you have a slipped disk.» She gave him a sarcastic smile and phoned the school. Florian nahm die Umschläge und verließ das Haus.

«Hello, Köder verläßt die Zentrale», Maddy informed Sakina and Manni. She was glad that she was at the *Zentrale* now and was no longer the bait. Let Florian see how he liked being in the hot seat. So Park was the first one to be spotted by Sakina.

They had given her that code-name because they had first noticed that she was watching them in the park. Well, Florian had noticed her in that pub first, really, but they first spoke about her in the park. It looked like she was one of the gang after all. Interesting, because they had all expected the man whom they had named *Spieß* to turn up first – they had named him after *drehen wir den Spieß um.* He was the one who had stolen her handbag and who could be seen clearly on the photo that Manni took at Wimbledon.

«Tennis an Zentrale», Mannis voice sounded very excited, «ich glaub, Spieß ist auch da, allerdings zusammen mit 'ner Frau. Herr und Frau Spieß. Ist ja 'ne richtige Vollversammlung. Over.»

Maddy passed on the information to Sakina. Spieß and a woman, maybe the partner who had brought the handbag back to the lost property office, or could that have been Park? Either way they knew now that there were at least three of them. It would make following them difficult. But with any luck they would stay together.

Florian fühlte sich ziemlich unwohl. Auffällig unauffällig ging er die High Road in Richtung Postamt entlang, die Versandtaschen gut sichtbar in der Hand. Ob Park ausgestiegen war und hinter ihm herlief? Oder langsam hinter ihm herfuhr? Ob Spieß aufgetaucht war? Er wollte sich liebend gern umdrehen, aber das durfte er natürlich nicht.

«Jasmin hier. Park ist noch im Auto. Was soll ich tun?»

«Stay put,» Maddy replied, «Tennis is, äh, ist bei Spieß.»

«Tennis an Zentrale», meldete sich Manni, «Köder ist kurz vor der Post. Die Spieße sind dicht hinter ihm, ungefähr 20 Meter.»

«Gut», answered Maddy and told him what she had heard from Sakina.

«Bloody hell!» That was Sakina again. «Park is getting out of her car and... sorry, sie geht zur High Road.»

«Du kriegst Besuch, Park kommt in deine Richtung.» That was Maddy to Manni, after she had told Sakina to follow Park at a safe distance.

Florian schwitzte. Er stand in einer langen Schlange, die sich unendlich langsam in Richtung Schalter bewegte. Ihm schien, als habe jeder Kunde tausend Extrawünsche. Was die anderen jetzt wohl machten? Ob die Verfolger schon hinter ihm in der Schlange warteten?

«Tennis an Zentrale, die Spieße stehen vor dem Schaufenster des Ladens neben der Post. Komisch, nicht, daß sie nicht hinter Köder reingegangen sind.»

How naive can you get, thought Maddy. Did Manni really think they would snatch the disks off Florian in broad daylight, in a busy post office, in front of loads of people?

«Hello Zentrale, this is urgent», Sakina called. «Park has just, ich meine, äh, oh to hell with it – she has just reached High Road but she's not walking towards the post office, she's heading in the other direction, towards the railway station. Maddy, what will I do?» Her voice sounded faint. She was moving out of the range of the walkie-talkies. «Just keep following her», Maddy screamed, «can you hear me?» There was no reply.

Endlich war Florian am Schalter angekommen. Er schob die Versandtaschen unter der Verglasung hindurch. Der Postmensch schob die Briefe zurück, murmelte irgendwas Unverständliches und zeigte auf die Waage, die vor dem Schalter stand. Aha. Selber wiegen, dachte Florian.

«Thirty-two for the London one and seventy each for the others», sagte der Mann und schob ihm die Briefmarken hin. Auch noch selber lecken muß man hier, dachte er, ein Service ist das! Als er endlich bezahlt und die frankierten Umschläge wieder unter der Verglasung durchgeschoben hatte, drehte er sich langsam um. Nichts, kein bekanntes Gesicht war zu sehen. Ob das alles umsonst war? Er ging zum Ausgang.

«Tennis, du bist jetzt on your own», said Maddy to Manni. She told him what had happened.

«Na toll, das hat uns gerade noch gefehlt. Und was mach ich, wenn mein spießiges Pärchen sich trennt? Moment», unterbrach er sich, «Köder kommt gerade aus dem Postamt.»

Those Germans, thought Maddy, always thinking in *ifs*. Why on earth should the *Spieße* split up? They were there to follow Florian.

«Ej, Zentrale», Manni klang verblüfft, «du wirst es nicht für möglich halten, Florian, äh, Köder geht die Straße runter, Herr Spieß geht in die entgegengesetzte Richtung zum Bahnhof und Frau Spieß ist einfach an der Bushaltestelle vor der Post stehengeblieben. Was nun?»

Maddy paused for a second. How odd. Maybe they thought that there was no point in following Florian any more now that the disks had been sent away. But Sakina, Manni and she should still keep track of the followers, even if they weren't following Florian any more. «Tennis», she decided, «you follow the man, I'll try to keep after the woman. The buses at that stop run quite infrequently. I'm sure she'll still be waiting when I get there. What does she look like? Over.»

Manni schaffte gerade noch eine Beschreibung der Frau,

bevor er in Richtung Bahnhof und außer Reichweite des Sprechgeräts lief. Jeder für sich allein, dachte er, so war das ja nicht geplant.

Florian fand nach zehn Minuten eine Telefonzelle und rief Maddy an. Aber die Zentrale antwortete nicht.

Siebtes Kapitel

in dem man nicht weiß, wer Fisch und wer Köder ist and in which shadows are shadowed

Drei Tage London. Drei Tage Wimbledon. Allen Leuten hatte er davon vorgeschwärmt. Und was war wirklich? Statt Asse, Top-Spins und Stops zu verfolgen, verfolgte er einen Mann im blauen Blazer. Erst durch das Gedränge in Wimbledon und jetzt auf dem Weg zum Bahnhof. Gut, daß er wenigstens dorthin ging. Und kein Auto dabei hatte. Wenn er bald herausbekommen könnte, wer der Mann war und wohin er ging, dachte Manni, wäre der Nachmittag in Wimbledon vielleicht doch noch zu retten. Sein Vater war am Abend zuvor ziemlich überrascht gewesen, als Manni ihm gesagt hatte, er hätte am nächsten Vormittag etwas anderes vor und würde den Weg nach Wimbledon später allein finden. Sie würden sich dann dort treffen. Es klappt auch bestimmt, munterte sich Manni auf.

Spieß stellte sich in der Schlange am Fahrkartenschalter an. Die stockte, weil an ihrer Spitze sich ein Mann beschwerte, daß er gerade den Zug nach West Norwood verpaßt hatte wegen des schleppenden Fahrkartenverkaufs.

Manni tat so, als lese er die Schlagzeilen der Zeitungen am Kiosk.

«Single to Waterloo, please», hörte er den Mann sagen. So wie er *Waterloo* sagte, klang das nach einem deutschen Akzent.

Manni zückte seine für das ganze Londoner Nahverkehrssystem gültige Tageskarte, eine *Capital Card*, auf die ihn sein Vater natürlich gleich bei der Ankunft in London hingewiesen hatte, und zeigte sie dem Fahrkartenkontrolleur. Kaum waren er und Spieß auf dem Bahnsteig, da fuhr auch schon der Zug ein.

Maddy sprinted out of the house, stopped, went back in, picked up her weekly Capital Card, and sprinted out again. Up the street she raced, until she got to the corner of High Road.

A few people were standing at the bus stop – a black woman with two young children, an old man wearing a plastic rain coat, and a punk. Fortunately there was only one woman there who fit the description Manni had given her. She saw that the bus was approaching. What should she do? Run after it? Would that look suspicious? Rubbish, she thought, people run after buses all the time.

Maddy ran, just managed to jump onto the open platform at the back of the bus as it was pulling away, breathed a sigh of relief, turned around and then froze. Frau Spieß was still standing at the bus stop.

Nach dem erfolglosen Anruf hatte Florian versucht, sich zu beruhigen. Sicher war Maddy als Zentrale so beschäftigt gewesen, Tennis und Jasmin zu koordinieren, daß sie es nicht geschafft hatte, ans Telefon zu gehen. Er schlenderte immer weiter die High Road entlang. Ein komisches Gefühl, wenn man nicht wußte, ob man beschattet wird und von wem. Er mußte bald mal die Gegend verlassen, damit er seine Schatten möglichst weit weg von Maddy führte.

Nach zehn Minuten kam er zum U-Bahnhof-Tooting Bec. Langsam ging er hinein und blieb lange vor dem großen Plan mit den verschiedenen Linien stehen. Er mußte schließlich Sakina und Manni Gelegenheit geben, zu den Schatten aufzuschließen.

Sakina felt quite nervous. She hoped she wouldn't bump into any friends of the family. Her parents thought she was in Maddy's house. They'd kill her if they knew what she was doing.

Park had gone into the Balham railway station and had bought a ticket to West Norwood. It took almost twenty minutes for the next train to arrive. Sakina felt quite exposed. There was nowhere much to hide. Even though the station was full, she kept thinking that Park must notice her.

I wouldn't fancy being followed by anyone, said Sakina to herself. Florian came to her mind – he was now the bait. Hopefully nothing would happen to him. She walked up and down the platform reading every poster on the wall at least twice. When the train arrived, she got in three carriages away from Park.

Spieß und Manni fuhren zwei Stationen bis Clapham Junction und stiegen um, Manni immer mit gehörigem Abstand. Am Bahnhof Waterloo ging der Mann direkt zum Taxistand und nahm das erste Taxi aus der Warteschlange. Manni erwischte das übernächste. Da man in London dem Taxifahrer vor dem Einsteigen das Fahrtziel angibt, meinte Manni sogar mitbekommen zu haben, was Herr Spieß gesagt hatte: Kings's Road oder so ähnlich. *King's Roads* gibt's in London sicher massenweise, dachte Manni, hier ist ja alles *royal*. Er wollte lieber auf Nummer Sicher gehen und nahm all seinen Mut zusammen.

«Could you follow that car, please», bat er seinen Taxifahrer und zeigte auf das Taxi mit Spieß, das an der Ampel warten mußte, «it's my uncle and...»

Er verhaspelte sich. Er wollte sagen, das ist mein Onkel, der hat gesagt, ich soll mit dem nächsten Taxi hinter ihm herfahren, und ich habe die Adresse vergessen und...

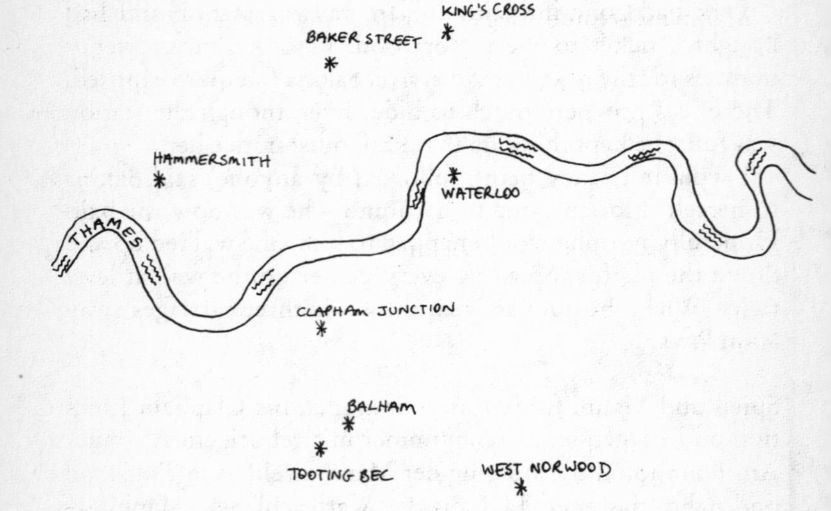

Der Taxifahrer sah ihn einen Moment verwirrt an, dann ging ein breites Grinsen über sein Gesicht.

«Follow that car, eh? Great stuff. Would you believe it, no one has ever said that to me before. Do you like the old movies and detective stories, then? I'm reading a good one at the moment, actually.»

Er zeigte auf ein Buch auf der Ablagefläche. *The Singing Detective* hieß es. «Oh yes, I'm a real fan of the old movies.»

Na, dann red doch nicht, sondern mach was, dachte Manni. Er fühlte sich wie auf glühenden Kohlen. Zum Glück stand das Taxi mit Spieß immer noch vor der roten Ampel.

«I thought you kids only went in for that Rambo stuff

nowadays», fuhr der Taxifahrer fort, «but the old ones were the really great films, where the hero would jump into a taxi and say ‹follow that car›. Well, hop in, young man – only if you've got enough money though.»

Manni nickte und stieg ein. Er hatte immerhin zwölf Pfund dabei.

«Follow that car, eh?» kicherte der Fahrer vor sich hin, als sie losfuhren.

Maddy was annoyed with herself. Why on earth hadn't she looked? Two different buses left from that stop, so she should have known that the woman mightn't have got into the first one. She got out at the next stop and ran part of the way back. Frau Spieß was still standing there. It would be a bit too obvious if she went back to the stop, Maddy thought, so she hung around in front of a pizza restaurant about a hundred yards away.

The next bus approached. It was a driver-only one, so it didn't have an open platform. She couldn't jump on this time. She walked towards the shop and got ready to run to get into the bus. But the woman didn't get in – Frau Spieß just stayed standing at the stop. To avoid looking too suspicious, Maddy walked straight on past her. After about fifty yards she stopped and turned around. The woman was just crossing the street. When she had reached the other side, she got into a car – a black Volvo – and drove off.

Maddy stood there gaping. Why hadn't she done that before? Why wait at a bus stop when you have a car? She looked up and down the street for a taxi. There's never a taxi in the south of London when you need one, her mother always said. And she was right. Not a taxi in sight. And the car had disappeared now, too. A depressed Maddy made her way home.

Florian stieg in die Northern Line ein und fuhr in Richtung Norden. Quietschend und rumpelnd bewegte sich der Zug vorwärts. Sicher ein Vorkriegsmodell, dachte er. Er sah sich in seinem Wagen um. Interessant, viel mehr Schwarze als Weiße im Zug. Keiner sah so aus, als sei er der Verfolger. Aber Verfolger, das wußte er aus allen Fernsehserien, sahen ja nie so aus, wie man sich das vorstellt. Er studierte den Streckenplan der Northern Line. Mist, die fuhr ja direkt durch King's Cross, genau da sollte er doch nicht hin.

In Waterloo stieg Florian deshalb in die Bakerloo Line um und schließlich in der Baker Street aus. Das ist weit genug weg, beschloß er. Als er aus dem U-Bahnhof kam, stand er fast direkt vor dem Eingang des Wachsfigurenkabinetts von Madame Tussaud. Das wär doch was, stellte er sich vor, eine wilde Verfolgung, er zwischen Hitler, Thatcher und Michael Jackson auf der Flucht vor seinen Beschattern. Aber er sollte ja nicht fliehen, und angeblich wußte er ja auch nicht, daß er beschattet wurde.

Er versuchte, sich unauffällig umzudrehen. Kein Verfolger zu sehen. Und auch von Sakina oder Manni keine Spur. Waren sie gut getarnt, oder hatten sie ihn und die Schatten verloren? Er beschloß, noch einmal zu versuchen, die Zentrale anzurufen.

When Park got out of the train at West Norwood, she walked up the stairs so briskly that Sakina had difficulty keeping up with her. Out of the station, she headed for the bus stop where a number 68 bus was waiting, and got into it. The bus pulled out immediately and Sakina was left standing on the pavement wondering what to do.

She didn't have to wonder long. Less than an minute later another 68 bus pulled up. Great, Sakina thought, maybe I will be able to catch up with her after all. She showed her ticket and went up the stairs. A front seat was empty. The bus drove off while the previous one was still in sight. Sakina breathed a sigh of relief.

«First time in Lonon, then?» fragte der Taxifahrer Manni.

Sie steckten im Verkehrsstau, aber das machte weiter nichts. Das Taxi mit Spieß stand nämlich auch, und zwischen beiden befanden sich etwa sechs Autos.

«Yes», antwortete Manni.

«Having a good time?»

«Oh yes, very exciting.» Das stimmte allemal.

«Been to see all the sights, have you?»

«Well, I've been to Wimbledon.»

«Lucky sod, I've never been there myself. Seen it on the box, but it's not really the same, is it.»

Sie fuhren weiter, immer dem ersten Taxi nach. Manni versuchte, sich zu merken, wo es langging, aber er erkannte fast gar nichts. Bloß das U-Bahn-Schild mit *Hammersmith* drauf. Daran vorbei fuhren sie, kurz bevor das Taxi von Spieß vor einem riesigen Bürogebäude anhielt, das ganz aus Glas gebaut zu sein schien. Über dem Haupteingang standen meterhohe, silbern glänzende Buchstaben: UNITED CHEMICALS. Spieß verschwand gerade durch den Haupteingang.

«That'll be nine pounds fifty», sagte der Fahrer, «and you'd better get a move on if you want to catch your – what did you say he was – your uncle? Funny that he didn't wait for you», er schaute Manni ins Gesicht, «or didn't he know you were following him?»

Manni sagte gar nichts, kramte das Geld hervor und gab dem Taxifahrer zehn Pfund.

«Happy hunting!» verabschiedete der sich.

Manni kaufte sich eine Zeitung und setzte sich auf eine

Bank, von der aus er den Eingang zu United Chemicals gut überblicken konnte.

Maddy was almost home now. She was still wondering about Frau Spieß. She looked to her right as she was about to cross the road and saw a green Fiat Uno parked a few yards away from her house. Sitting in the driver's seat was a young man, a sporty type, with curly blond hair. He was talking on the car telephone.

My God, thought Maddy, how many of them are there? When she got home, the phone was ringing.

Die ersten drei Telefonzellen, die Florian fand, waren kaputt. Die vierte akzeptierte nur Kreditkarten oder eine *Phonecard*. Wütend ging er in den nächsten Laden und kaufte eine. Seine Laune besserte sich auch nicht, als er von Maddy, die gerade nach Hause kam, erfuhr, was passiert war, seit er die Post verlassen hatte.

«Heißt das, daß mich überhaupt keiner verfolgt hat», fragte er entgeistert, «das ganze Rumgeschaukle in der Stinkebahn war alles umsonst?»

«The what?» Maddy asked, «that was all double-dutch to me.»

«I was just praising your wonderful London Transport. Did no one follow me at all, then?»

«It doesn't look like it,» Maddy had to admit, «unless you were being shadowed by people who we haven't spotted at all yet, but somehow I doubt that.»

«Ok», antwortete Florian und klang auf einmal sehr müde, «dann komme ich aber auch mit zum Bahnhof King's Cross.»

«Fine, it's a bit early, but there's not much point in hanging around here. I think I'll leave now. I'll meet you at whatever platform the train from Edinburgh arrives at.» Maddy left the house and went to the station. Florian ging zum U-Bahnhof zurück.

Sakina was feeling pleased with herself. The worst thing that could happen now would be that Park would get out of the bus, and that Sakina would not be able to stop her bus in time, but would have to get out at the next stop and run back. But that was no problem at all. She hadn't won the mile race at school for nothing. She sat back and felt quite optimistic.

Both buses had passed by two stops without halting so far. The first bus was about a hundred yards ahead of the second one. The indicator flashed to show that it was going to stop. Sakina saw Park getting out. She ran downstairs and pressed the bell. Too late, the bus didn't stop. The next stop wasn't too far away. She pressed the bell again. The bus just sailed past it. She pressed the bell two, three, four times and nothing happened.

«He won't stop, love, no matter how many times you press that bell,» said an old man sitting next to the door. Sakina felt like she was in some weird film. Why wouldn't the bus stop?

«Didn't you see the number on the front when you got in?» the old man asked her. «This is not your normal 68, it's the X68, non-stop from West Norwood to Waterloo and then stopping at all stops to King's Cross. Very quick way of getting into the centre. Great invention. But he won't stop for anyone before he gets to Waterloo.»

Manni verbrachte einige Zeit vor dem Gebäude der United Chemicals. Gut, daß englische Tageszeitungen so dick sind, daß man tatsächlich eine Stunde in ihnen lesen könnte, dachte er, gute Tarnung. Wirklich gelesen hatte er allerdings nur die

Sportseite; nicht gerade die reine Freude, stand doch dort, was er gestern in Wimbledon alles verpaßt hatte.

Um wieviel Uhr sollte der Zug von der Cousine ankommen? Dreizehn Uhr acht. Bis dahin, so lautete sein Auftrag, sollte er Spieß im Auge behalten. Wenn in der nächsten halben Stunde nichts passierte, dann ging es ab nach Wimbledon.

Fünf Minuten später kam Spieß die Treppe herunter. Er ging zum Straßenrand und wartete. Schnell lief Manni schräg über die Straße. So war er auf der gleichen Straßenseite und konnte, wenn nötig, an Spieß vorbeigehen. Ein großer schwarzer Volvo fuhr vor. Die Scheibe wurde heruntergelassen.

«He's followed her to King's Cross», hörte Manni Spieß sagen.

Die hintere Tür wurde geöffnet. «Get in», kam die Stimme einer Frau aus dem Wageninneren.

In Mannis Kopf hämmerte es, seine Knie zitterten. Also hatten die Maddy beschattet und nicht umgekehrt. Manni zählte sein Geld. Noch gerade zwei Pfund. Kein *follow that car*-Taxitrip mehr. Er rannte zur U-Bahn. Hoffentlich gibt es nur Staus für die Autos, betete er, hoffentlich kommt gleich 'ne U-Bahn, hoffentlich kann ich Maddy noch warnen, hoffentlich.

Chapter Eight

in which the battle of King's Cross takes place und in dem sich ein paar Zufälle zu viel ereignen

«Oh great, there you are,» Sakina had just spotted Florian and Maddy. She was still furious that she had hopped into the express bus to Waterloo and King's Cross. Florian and Maddy blickten Sakina leicht entgeistert an. Wieso war sie hier? Hoffentlich hatte sie nicht unfreiwillig Park mitgebracht. Gleichzeitig freute Florian sich jedoch. Er mochte sie ganz gern, sie war irgendwie ganz anders als Maddy.

Sakina told them about the surprising end of her tailing of Park.

«Oh well,» Maddy said when she was finished. «If she got out three stops after West Norwood, and you were in the express bus, at least she can't have followed you to us. Anyway, it's not all that bad if there are three of us here.»

«And maybe Manni has found out where *Herr Spieß* went, who he is or who he works for,» Sakina added.

Umsteigen. Manni überholte alle Leute auf der Rolltreppe. Sorry. Sorry. Sorry. Er jagte die Gänge entlang, die im U-Bahnhof Victoria die District- und die Victoria-Line verbinden. Schneller. Schneller. Er mußte in King's Cross ankommen, bevor der Zug aus Edinburgh die Diskette zu Maddy und damit auch direkt zu den Spießen und ihren Partnern brachte.

Neither Maddy, Sakina nor Florian could make head or tail of Park's behaviour. And when Maddy went on to tell Sakina about Frau Spieß waiting at the bus stop only to drive off in a car in the end, none of them could come up with a good reason for that either.

Victoria – Green Park – Oxford Circus – Warren Street. Tür auf, Menschen drängeln raus, Menschen drängeln rein, Tür zu, langsames Anfahren, Halt auf der Strecke. Dabei war doch gar keine *rush-hour*.

Die fünf Stationen bis zu King's Cross schienen Manni eine Ewigkeit zu dauern. Er blickte auf seine Uhr. 13.06. Endlich rollte die U-Bahn in King's Cross ein.

Manni jagte die Treppen hinauf, immer dem British-Rail-Zeichen hinterher, überholte die Schlange an der Fahrkartenkontrolle, achtete nicht auf die mißbilligenden Blicke der Engländer, zeigte dem Kontrolleur im Vorbeidrängeln seine Karte und stürmte die Treppen hoch, zum Eisenbahnbahnhof.

13.08. The train from Edinburgh arrived on time. «Pünktlich wie die Bundesbahn», konnte es sich Florian nicht verkneifen zu sagen, denn er hatte Maddy und Mrs. Butler lange genug über unpünktliche englische Züge schimpfen hören. Seiner von der Fähre zum Londoner Bahnhof Liverpool Street war auch erst mit knapp einer Stunde Verspätung angekommen.

Janet was one of the first to get out of the train. «Maddy!» she exclaimed, and gave her cousin a big hug, «lovely to see you again so soon. Here, I've brought something along for you,» she said while rummaging around in her bag.

Florian verliebte sich sofort, nicht in Janet, die außerdem bestimmt sechs oder sieben Jahre älter war als er, sondern in ihren Akzent. Wie anders der klang als alles, was er bisher gehört hatte. So sprachen also Schotten.

Endlich. Manni hatte die Bahnhofshalle erreicht. Ganz schön groß dafür, daß das nur einer von vielen Londoner Bahnhöfen war. Wo zum Teufel kam der Zug aus Edinburgh an? Die hatten hier keine weißen Ankunftstafeln wie zu Hause.

Aha, stand nicht dahinten Florian. Wieso Florian? Und Sakina?! Verrückt!

Janet found the box with the disks and handed it over to Maddy. Maddy was just going to introduce Florian and Sakina to her cousin when it happened. It was all over very soon, but at the time Maddy felt she was seeing it happen in slow motion.

«Janet, this is...» Maddy began when she suddenly felt an arm closing around her throat. She could hardly breathe. What was going on?

«Just keep your mouth shut and nothing will happen to you,» she heard a woman's voice say quietly in her ear, «but any funny tricks and you'll be sorry,» she threatened.

Maddy could see Florian gasping for breath while Herr Spieß had him in a strangle-hold. A man with a moustache whom she had never seen before was holding Sakina, who had turned deadly pale. The attackers had their arms around them

O nein, da war Frau Spieß. Und Herr Spieß. Wie aus der Luft gezaubert standen die beiden plötzlich hinter Maddy und Florian. Und ein Mann mit einem Schnurrbart, wohl der *Er*, von dem Frau Spieß gesagt hatte, daß er Maddy beschattete, tauchte hinter Sakina auf. Manni konnte es nicht fassen. Er war noch nicht einmal dreißig Meter von ihnen entfernt. Dreißig Meter zu spät für eine Warnung.

Die Spieße und der Mann hatten jeder einen Arm so um Maddys, Florians und Sakinas Hals gelegt, daß sie ihnen jederzeit die Luft abschnüren konnten. Aber sie taten das

in such a way that it did not look suspicious, no one near by came to help them – it must have looked like they were all embracing each other, which is not an unusual thing for people to do at a railway station. Maddy felt sick. How the hell did they know ...?

«I'll take that, thank you very much.» The moustached man holding Sakina grabbed the box of disks off Maddy. Janet stood rooted to the spot like a frightened rabbit. Get help, Janet, Maddy thought, but Janet just stood there.

The man with the disks in his hand let Sakina go and started to move away when a young man with blond curly hair ran full speed into him, bringing his arm upwards with such force against the one holding the disks that, while the man with the moustache was falling to the ground, the box flew into the air. Maddy wanted to run after it, but the arm held against her throat pressed even harder. She followed

so geschickt, daß es für einen flüchtigen Passanten wie eine ungelenke Umarmung aussah. Neben Maddy stand eine junge Frau mit einer Reisetasche – die mußte wohl die Cousine sein – bei ihr stand keiner, aber sie war wohl so verblüfft, daß sie so schnell gar nicht auf die Idee kam, ihnen zu Hilfe zu kommen.

Der Typ mit dem Schnurrbart ließ Sakina los, griff nach der Diskettenbox, die die Cousine Maddy übergeben hatte, und setzte dazu an wegzulaufen. Die Spieße hielten Maddy und Florian noch fest umklammert. Manni blieb stehen und sah wie hypnotisiert zu der Gruppe hinüber.

Kaum hatte sich der Mann mit der Box in Bewegung gesetzt, da wurde er von einem Passanten, einem jungen Mann mit blondem, lockigen Haar so heftig angerempelt, daß er umfiel. Dabei schlug der Blonde ihm mit dem Unterarm so gegen das Handgelenk, daß die Diskettenbox durch die Luft flog, auf

the box with her eyes. Was that, could that possibly be Manni running towards it? Please God let it be him, Maddy prayed.

«Oh, I'm awfully sorry», the blond man said as he helped the fallen man to his feet, «I wasn't looking where I was going.» He seemed to be holding on tightly to his arm. At the same time a lady with a heavy suitcase walked straight into Herr Spieß.

«A thousand apologies,» she said before walking on.

Herr Spieß had lost his balance though, and Florian managed to free himself.

It's now or never, thought Maddy, feeling the arm loosening around her throat. She grabbed the arm of the surprised woman – it was Frau Spieß as Maddy could now see – and threw her over her shoulder onto the ground. She had always known that her Judo training would come in handy some day. The man with the moustache who had grabbed the box of disks before losing it again was now running to retrieve

Manni zu. «Oh, sorry», sagte der Blonde und half dem Mann auf, hielt ihn dabei aber noch am Arm fest. Gleichzeitig wurde Herr Spieß von einer Frau mit einem schweren Koffer so gestreift, daß er für einen Moment die Balance verlor und Florian sich ihm entwinden konnte. Und Frau Spieß wurde offensichtlich eine Sekunde später von Maddy mit einem Griff zu Boden geschleudert, sehr zur Verblüffung einer etwas älteren Frau, die urplötzlich hinter ihnen auftauchte und, so schien es Manni jedenfalls, mit ihrem Gepäck-Trolly geradewegs in Frau Spieß hineinfahren wollte. Sakina und die Cousine standen einfach da, Florian und Maddy entwanden sich den Spießen, der Mann mit dem Schnurrbart war gerade dabei, von dem Passanten, der ihn angerempelt hatte, loszukommen. Jetzt oder nie, dachte Manni, also jetzt.

Er rannte auf die Diskettenbox zu, ebenso wie der Mann mit dem Schnurrbart,

it once more. Maddy could see Manni – it was definitely him – running towards the box, too. The man was almost there, when out of the blue an elderly woman with a luggage trolly appeared straight in the middle of his path. He fell over it, arms und legs in all directions, and landed on the ground.

«I'm so sorry,» said the old lady sweetly as she helped him to his feet, «terribly sorry.»

Manni had managed by this time to grab the box and run. Maddy, now free, and Janet, still dazed but dragged along by Maddy, ran towards him.

«Zu mir nach Hause», shouted Maddy after him, «run!»

Florian and Sakina just stood there, eyes wide, mouth open, and watched.

der sich endlich aufgerappelt und von dem Passanten losgerissen hatte. Doch der Mann kam nicht weit, denn die Frau mit dem Gepäck-Trolly, die einen Augenblick zuvor fast Maddy und Frau Spieß angefahren hätte, fuhr ihm direkt in den Weg, so daß er über den Wagen stolperte.

«I am so sorry, terribly sorry», murmelte die alte Dame und half ihm beim Aufstehen.

So viele Zufälle gibt es auf der Welt nicht, dachte Manni, als er im Laufen die Diskettenbox aufhob.

«Zu mir nach Hause», rief Maddy ihm nach, «run!»

Er sah sich kurz um. Sakina und Florian standen noch da. Maddy rannte zum Ausgang und zog die völlig perplexe Cousine mit ihrer schweren Umhängetasche hinter sich her. Manni rannte zur U-Bahn, die Diskettenbox fest unter den Arm geklemmt.

Neuntes Kapitel

in dem ein ungeordneter Rückzug stattfindet and in which the return to base is followed by a suspicious visitor

Manni sprang in den nächsten U-Bahn-Zug, egal wohin.

Maddy, with the still totally perplexed Janet in tow, jumped onto the next bus which came along. It was going to Waterloo.

Sakina und Florian sahen, wie die Spieße und der Mann mit dem Schnurrbart Manni und Maddy zum Ausgang hinterher rannten. Sie blieben einfach erst mal stehen. Die Leute, die Spieß und Co. in die Quere gekommen waren, schienen sich in Luft aufgelöst zu haben.

For a moment during the action Sakina had thought that one of them, the elderly woman with the suitcase, looked a bit like Park. Oh no, she thought, I'm beginning to see things.

Florian atmete tief durch. Er verstand das alles nicht. Dieser plötzliche Überfall, dann die Häufung von zufälligen Störungen, die die Angreifer durcheinandergebracht hatten, die Verfolgerei und Ablenkerei am Morgen, die offensichtlich nicht geklappt hatte, das paßte alles überhaupt nicht zusammen.

«What will we do now?» fragte er Sakina, während sie langsam den Bahnhof verließen, «go to the Butler's house?»

«If I was one of the people after the disk, that's the first place I'd go to.»

Da hatte sie recht. Hoffentlich liefen Manni und Maddy denen nicht noch auf diese Weise in die Arme. «Let's go and have a burger and think about it», schlug er vor und zeigte auf den Wimpy-Laden auf der anderen Straßenseite. Sakina made a face. «I don't eat meat,» she said, «but I'll join you for a strawberry shake.»

Maddy and Janet got the bus to Waterloo. Maddy wanted to get home quickly and Janet had an interview for a job that afternoon. But they managed to talk a bit on the bus. Maddy told her cousin a very brief version of what had happened over the last few days.

«I'm sorry I didn't warn you how explosive the disk was», she apologized, «but I thought if I told the story to Auntie Dorothy, she wouldn't send it down at all, and most certainly not with you. Sorry about the scene at the station, too, we really did our best to try to fool them into not following us there», she sighed, «but they are obviously a lot cleverer than we are.»

Janet laughed. «What do you expect!»

Maddy said they would take the disk to the police now. The whole thing had got out of hand.

Janet was going to spend a few days in London and was staying with another aunt of theirs who lived there.

«If Florian wasn't here, you'd be staying with us,» grumbled Maddy, who liked her cousin a lot.

«Never mind,» replied Janet. «He seems to be nice enough – the bit I saw of him. Do you get on well together?»

«Alright, not brilliant,» was the muttered answer.

«Look,» Maddy said as they got out of the bus, «I'll ring you tomorrow and let you know what's happening – and to find out how your interview went. Good luck,» she added.

«Thanks.»

Maddy ran into the station. The next train via Clapham Junction was leaving in two minutes.

Zum Glück fuhr die U-Bahn, in die Manni blindlings gestiegen war, gar nicht so eine ungünstige Strecke. Sie hielt als nächstes in Euston, wo er die U-Bahn nach Balham nehmen konnte. Er sah sich beim Umsteigen genau um, aber er konnte niemanden entdecken, der ihm folgte. Er hatte die Diskettenbox fest an sich gedrückt. So schnell wie möglich kopieren und ab zur Polizei mit dem Ding, die Spieß-Gesellen kommen bestimmt auch auf die Idee, zu Maddys Haus zu fahren, dachte er. Die Hoffnung, daß er es an diesem Nachmittag doch noch nach Wimbledon schaffen würde, schwand, während die Northern Line in Richtung Süden fuhr. Zwischen Waterloo und Kennington hielt der Zug mitten im Tunnel. Verstohlen musterte Manni die Leute in seinem Wagen. Alle blickten teilnahmslos vor sich hin.

Florian und Sakina hatten einen freien Tisch gefunden und die ganze Geschichte noch einmal durchdiskutiert. «It doesn't make sense,» was Sakina's comment on the whole thing, «it just doesn't.»

Beide zogen an ihrem Strohhalm im Erdbeer-Shake.

«Well», begann Florian, «I think you are very nice. Do you want to go to a disco with me when this silly computer business is over?»

Das klingt bestimmt schrecklich, dachte er. Viel zu direkt. Nicht so direkt, Kinder, hatte der Schwatske immer gesagt, in England ist man nicht so direkt. Florian konnte so was schon auf deutsch nicht richtig rausbringen. Und dann erst auf englisch!

Sakina blushed. «Thank you, that's very nice of you,» she smiled and said, «but I don't think that will be possible. My family wouldn't allow me. Asian families are different in that respect, you know.»

Einen langen Moment sagte keiner etwas. Then Sakina looked at her watch.

«I'm afraid I have to go now,» she said, «I have to look after my little brothers most afternoons.» She got up to leave.

«I'll, äh, I'll phone you», stotterte Florian, «I mean, to tell you what happened to the disk.»

Sakina smiled and pushed her hair back off her face.

«You don't have to do that,» she said, «I can come around to Maddy's tomorrow and you can tell me then.»

Nachdem sie gegangen war, stand Florian auf, ging zurück zum Bahnhof und nahm sich ein Taxi. Zu irgendwas mußte das Geld, das ihm seine Mutter gegeben hatte, ja gut sein. Wenn Maddy dabei war, wollte er nicht Taxi fahren, die hätte dafür kein Verständnis. *Rich kid* sagte sie sowieso schon oft genug zu ihm. So aber genoß er es, in dem großen schwarzen Wagen durch London chauffiert zu werden.

Nachdem der Zug über fünf Minuten im Tunnel steckte und keine Anzeichen machte, weiterzufahren, kam langsam Stimmung auf im Wagen. Manni erinnerte sich an einen Film, der in der Berliner U-Bahn spielte, *Linie 1*, den er vor kurzem gesehen hatte. Da hatten sich auch alle stumm gegenübergesessen und dann plötzlich einen Song angestimmt. Toll war das gewesen.

«Typical bloody Northern Line», sagte der Typ neben ihm, «they treat their passengers so badly. No wonder that they get hijacked.»

«Hijacked? The tube?» fragte Manni verwundert.

«Yeah, didn't you hear about it? There were quite a few hijacks of Northern Line tubes about two months ago. I was on one of them. We had been waiting so long for the tube, and when it finally came, an announcement was made saying it would not be going further than about two or three stops.

Everyone just decided that it wasn't good enough, and stood in the way of the doors so they couldn't shut. The driver could do nothing until he said he'd drive the whole way. People should do it more often in protest about the bad service. The Northern Line is worst of all.»

Jeder hatte eine Geschichte über die Northern Line zu erzählen, und keine davon war positiv. Immerhin ein schöner Zeitvertreib, dachte Manni. Es dauerte noch weitere fünf Minuten, bis sich der Zug wieder in Bewegung setzte.

Mannis U-Bahn und Maddys Zug kamen fast gleichzeitig in Balham an, und so stießen die beiden am Ausgang aufeinander.

Maddy breathed a sigh of relief when she saw him. «Are you ok?» she asked.

«Fine, are you?»

«Yeah. I don't think anyone was following me, was anyone after you?»

«No, but I think they will äh...»

«They will be watching our house, you mean?» Maddy finished his sentence.

Manni nickte. Computerexperten verstanden sich eben blind.

«Don't worry, I've thought of that already. There's a door in the fence at the back of our garden. Behind it is a narrow path and on the other side of the path is the door into the Mulligan's garden. The Mulligan's house is in the next street parallel to ours and there's a side entrance into their garden. We're very friendly with them and I often used to go home that way as a kid.»

Manni folgte Maddy durch den Nachbargarten und den eigenen Garten ins Haus.

«Good that Mum never locks that door into the garden,» she grinned.

They rushed upstairs and switched on the computer.

«Safety copy first and then to the police, I suppose,» said Maddy while the computer went through its initial routine.

Manni nickte. Genau das hatte er auch gedacht. «Let's have a DIR first», schlug er vor, «so that we can see what's on it.»

Als das Taxi von der High Road abbog, sah Florian, wie eine Frau gerade auf das Haus der Butlers zuging. Er beugte sich vor.

«Excuse me», rief er durch die Glasscheibe, die den Fahrgast vom Fahrer trennt, «I told you the wrong number. I want to go to that house down there with the ‹For sale› sign.» Er deutete auf ein Schild, das ungefähr fünfzig Meter vom Butlerschen Haus entfernt war.

Der Taxifahrer nickte und fuhr weiter.

So kann ich erst mal von hinten herankommen und sehen, wer das ist, dachte Florian, stieg aus und bezahlte.

‹DIR A:› Maddy keyed, in order to see the directory of the disk.

```
Volume in drive A has no label
Directory of A:

INTRO      DOC        7428    01.01.88  10.01
ADDRESS    DBF      102444    01.01.88  10.01


           2 File(s)  260064 bytes free



C>
```

Maddy and Manni looked at each other in disappointment. «Just a WORD and a DBASE file,» Maddy exclaimed.

So was Popeliges, dachte Manni. Nach all der Verfolgerei hatte er etwas völlig anderes erwartet, irgend etwas verschlüsselt Programmiertes oder wenigstens exotische Software, aber nicht etwas in kommerzieller Software, die jeder benutzte.

«A bit of an anti-climax, isn't it,» said Maddy. «Oh well, I suppose it's the contents that matter and not the beauty of the program.»

«Ich vermute.. äh, you have DBASE and WORD», sagte Manni, der Maddy zutraute, daß sie bei der Software-Beschaffung genauso erfolgreich war wie er und seine Freunde in Berlin.

«You assume rightly,» she laughed, «a little birdy just dropped it onto my windowsill.» She called up the subdirectory of her hard disk which contained WORD.

Manni wollte gerade fragen, was ein Vögelchen damit zu tun hatte, als es klingelte.

Maddy and Manni jumped up and went to the window. They peeped out from behind the curtain. At the door was a woman in her forties, holding up a copy of *Watchtower*, the pamphlet of the Jehova Witnesses. Maddy suddenly felt weak. There was no mistaking it: the woman was Park in disguise.

Chapter Ten

in which a visit to the police brings some surprises und in dem Florian geheimnisvollen Anweisungen folgt

Quick as a shot, Maddy pulled Manni away from the window. «It's Park,» she said. She went over to the computer and took the disk out of the disk drive. «Come on, we've got to get out of here quickly.» They left through the garden, the same way they had come in only a few minutes earlier.

Die Frau wartete einige Augenblicke vor dem Haus und ging dann zurück in Richtung High Road. Florian folgte in weitem Abstand; wenn ihn nicht alles täuschte, war diese Frau Park. Sie bog in die High Road ein und ging sie hinunter. Florian überlegte einen Moment, dann folgte er ihr.

They ran as fast as they could and were pretty much out of breath when they arrived at the police station.

«Oh God, not him again,» panted Maddy as soon as they got inside. She nodded towards a policeman who was reading a newspaper. «It's that bald police constable, remember, the one who didn't take my story about the missing container of disks very seriously. He will probably throw me out as soon as I say the word *computer.*»

«Egal, wir müssen's versuchen, zurück ins Haus können wir nicht», meinte Manni.

Maddy took a deep breath and stepped forward.

«Hello Maddy,» said the policeman, laying his newspaper to one side, «how nice of you to call in again so soon. Is this your friend Florian?»

«No, that's Manni,» she replied automatically before it occurred to her how strange his behaviour was. How did he remember her name? Why wasn't he annoyed to see her again? And how on earth did he know Florian's name? She didn't think she had mentioned it to him when she was there to get the container fingerprinted. She was very puzzled.

The policeman laughed at the expression on her face. «It's alright», he said, «all will be revealed soon. Just step in there and wait a moment.» He pointed down the corridor to the first door on the left, «Inspector McGregor will be right with you.»

Die Frau ging jetzt ziemlich schnell. Florian hinterher. Einmal drehte sie sich um. Er meinte zu sehen – obwohl das bei dem Abstand nicht so eindeutig festzustellen war –, daß sie plötzlich lächelte. Hatte sie ihn entdeckt? Wußte sie, wer er war?

«Young man, I think you just dropped this.» Ein blonder Mann tippte ihm auf die Schulter und hielt ihm einen Briefumschlag hin. Florian wollte gerade *No* sagen, als er las, was darauf geschrieben stand: *FLORIAN – READ ME NOW!* Völlig durcheinander nahm er den Umschlag und murmelte: «Thanks.»

The door opened. All of a sudden Maddy's eyes widened and she turned very pale. Hands clenched into fists, fists pulled up against her cheeks, she opened her mouth to let out a scream which would have woken the dead.

«AAAAAAAAAGH!» Maddy schrie, als hätte sie ein Gespenst gesehen. Dabei war bloß ein Mann ins Zimmer gekommen, wahrscheinlich dieser Inspektor McGregor.

«Yes Maddy, your eyes are working properly and no, I'm not a ghost», sagte er, «I'm Inspector McGregor and I'm also the man you think is dead.»

Der Blonde ging weiter. So ruhig, wie das mit zitternden Fingern möglich war, versuchte Florian, den Zettel aus dem Briefumschlag zu holen und ihn im Gehen zu lesen. Die Notiz war offensichtlich in großer Eile geschrieben und schwer zu entziffern.

Florian –

Please dont worry.

This has been handed to you by
a police officer.

We think that someone might be
following you
Stop shadowing the woman.
Turn left at the supermarket,
then right, right again;
then take the second turn to the right,
start running to shake off possible
followers.
Turn left, left again
and then right.
The first gate on the left hand side
is the back entrance to the police
station.
Go in and ask for Inspector McGregor.

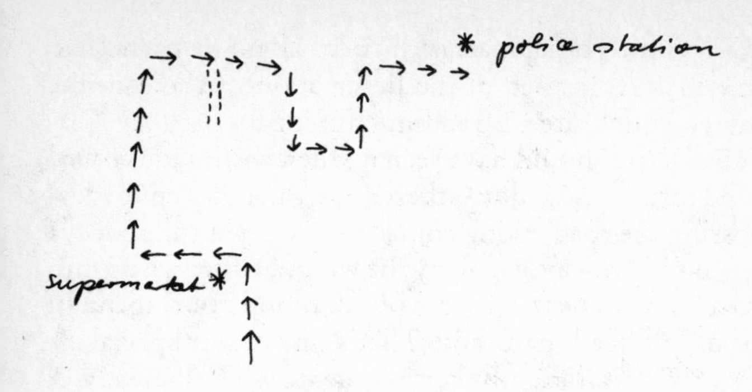

Florian sah sich um. Alles sah so normal aus. Ein roter Doppeldeckerbus kroch durch den Verkehr, Mütter mit Kinderwagen gingen einkaufen, ein paar ältere Leute standen an der nächsten Ecke neben dem fliegenden Blumenhändler – wer sollte ihn beobachten? Wie im Traum folgte er den Anweisungen. Am Supermarkt links, dann rechts, noch mal rechts, eine auslassen, wieder rechts, spurten, links rein, gleich wieder links, das waren ja wirklich schnelle Abbiegungen, noch einmal rechts rum. Er war da.

«Hello Florian», hörte er jemanden sagen. Am Tor stand ein Polizist mit Glatze.

«But… but… the story and the picture in the paper…» stuttered Maddy.

«All part of a necessary show», said Inspector McGregor.

«So there was no accident.» Maddy was beginning to recover from the shock and come to her senses again.

«Oh yes there was, a highly spectacular one. I pride myself on being a bit of a stuntman you know, and a good friend of mine from the police training school and I have a routine that would do a James Bond film proud. You've seen it, haven't you, Jimmy?»

Jimmy was the young man with curly blond hair who had just come in. He grinned at the description of the routine. «Well, maybe not quite a Bond film, but it isn't bad.»

«Isn't bad! You should have seen it when we did it in Edinburgh», he turned to Maddy, «there I was, an innocent pedestrian crossing the road, along comes the Passat at full speed, I try to run out of the way, get hit by the wing, am thrown up into the air and land in a heap on the ground. Blood pouring out of the back of my head, naturally. That's one of our special effects. In no time at all an ambulance comes to whisk me away. A couple of days later I am dead. It's a routine my friend Douglas and I have had a lot of practice in. And it works well every time.» Jimmy, the blond policeman, nodded in agreement.

Moment mal, dachte Manni, Jimmy war doch auf dem Bahnhof, oder? Das war der, der den Mann mit dem Schnurrbart angerempelt und ihm die Diskettenbox aus der Hand geschlagen hatte. Also waren das keine gesammelten Zufälle am Bahnhof. Sie hatten Polizeiunterstützung gehabt. Aber warum dann das ganze Theater, warum hatten sie Spieß und seine Kumpane nicht einfach festgenommen?

Maddy was just thinking that the blond policeman looked very much like the fellow who had got into Park's green car after she had made her way to West Norwood. In fact, she could have sworn that it was the same man. But it didn't make much sense.

«He's on his way here now,» Maddy heard Jimmy say under his breath to the inspector.

«So you are not dead. That's nice,» Maddy tried to organize her thoughts, «but that's the only thing I am sure about at the moment.»

«That's not surprising,» the inspector said as he took a pipe out of his jacket pocket, «but all will be revealed in a moment when everybody is here.»

Who is *everybody*, Maddy wondered. Would Grandad turn up next?

Kitsch, komm raus, du bist umzingelt, dachte Manni, jetzt raucht der doch tatsächlich Pfeife; nach Sherlock Holmes kann sich das ein echter Detektiv doch gar nicht mehr leisten.

Es klopfte. Der kahle Polizist steckte den Kopf durch die Tür und sagte: «A visitor, sir.» Er schob Florian in den Raum.

«Mensch, Florian», rief Manni. Er und Maddy sprangen gleichzeitig auf.

«Wieso seid ihr denn hier?» fragte Florian. «Habt ihr etwa auch so 'n Brief bekommen?»

«Was für 'n Brief?» fragte Manni zurück.

Schnell berichtete Florian, wie er zur Polizei gefunden hatte. Die Taxifahrt ließ er lieber weg. «Und wieso seid ihr hier?» fragte er dann noch einmal.

Instead of answering his question Maddy asked him one: «Aren't you surprised about anything else? Take a look around.»

Florian sah sich um. Der blonde Mann lächelte ihn an. Den hatte er erwartet. «Thanks for the letter», wollte er ganz lokker sagen, aber seine Stimme vibrierte vor lauter Aufregung.

«Don't mention it», gab Jimmy zurück, «all in the line of duty.»

Florians Blick fiel auf den Mann, der in seiner Pfeife stocherte. Nee, das kann nicht sein, das geht ja nicht, durchfuhr es ihn, der ist doch tot. Aber der Mann sah tatsächlich so aus wie der Mann auf dem Foto in der Zeitung, wie der Detektiv, der an allem schuld war. Florian wurde ganz anders zumute.

«Yes, Florian,» said the man seeing the blood draining out of Florian's face, «it's me – Inspector McGregor alias Gordon Mackey, short term carrier of a box of disks, and corpse after an accident.» Er versuchte wieder, die Pfeife anzuzünden.

Kein Wunder, daß Detektive Pfeife rauchen, dachte

Manni, so können sie sich beim Nichtstun und Nichtssagen beschäftigen, während alle anderen immer aufgeregter werden.

Die Tür ging nochmals auf. «Oh no!» Maddy heard Florian und Manni groan at the same time as herself. And no wonder. Coming into the room was Park.

«It's about time, Yardley,» said Inspector McGregor and put his pipe on the table, «as you can see, they found their own way here.»

Elftes Kapitel

in dem viel enthüllt wird but nothing is solved

«I expect you know Inspector Yardley already, even though you have never actually met her properly», sagte McGregor. Florian meinte, dabei einen spöttischen Unterton herausgehört zu haben. Kein Wunder, wenn man jemanden beschattet, sollte man von dem auch nicht gesehen werden. Nur – wenn sie zur Polizei gehörte und nicht zu den Spießen, wieso hatte diese Frau Yardley sie dann überhaupt beobachtet?

«I think we owe you an explanation and an apology,» said McGregor. You can say that again, thought Maddy.

His face took on a serious look. «You two are German, aren't you?» wandte er sich an Manni und Florian. Die nickten. «I'm sorry I don't speak your language, but I suppose your English is good. Please interrupt me though, if there's anything you don't understand.» Er holte seine Pfeife vom Tisch und fing erneut an, in ihr herumzustochern. Nun leg endlich los, dachte Florian.

«Inspector Yardley and I have been working together with two computer specialists on a case of large-scale computer fraud. I believe that you are very well versed in computers,» McGregor addressed the three of them.

Florian sah, wie Manni und Maddy nickten. Ja, die beiden kannten sich mit Computern aus. Computer! Florian konnte es immer noch nicht so richtig fassen, daß ausgerechnet er, der sich fest vorgenommen hatte, nie so alberne Computer-Spiele zu spielen und nie was mit dieser Kiste zu tun haben zu müssen, seit drei Tagen nur noch mit Disketten und Computer-Verrückten beschäftigt war.

«Fine», war der Inspektor inzwischen fortgefahren, «that makes things easier. So, we were working on this big fraud case in which millions of pounds were disappearing from different banks all over the world and reappearing, via several detours, in carefully disguised accounts. Whoever it was, was finding his way into the programs used by the banks to transfer money internationally, and diverting money to any one of many accounts they had set up. You can believe me, an ordinary bank-robbery is child's play compared to this game.»

Florian konnte sich nicht so richtig vorstellen, wie man mit Hilfe von Computern Geld klauen konnte. Wie das wohl funktionierte? Die haben Geld von verschiedenen Konten abgezweigt und auf andere umgeleitet, das war leicht zu verstehen. Aber wie kann man dabei unentdeckt bleiben? Als Florian merkte, daß Manni und Maddy fasziniert zuhörten, fragte er erst mal nicht.

«The whole thing was covered up very well. We worked for months without results, even though we knew that one of the centres had to be somewhere here in London. You see, there are no fingerprints involved in this kind of crime, no tools, no secret meetings at midnight, and it's all so damned fast. You can imagine how frustrating it was. After about four months we finally had a lead – nothing that could be proven, but at least we had a suspect – an accountant...»

«From United Chemicals», unterbrach Manni ihn stolz. Er mußte das Ergebnis seiner Jagd durch Wimbledon und der Taxifahrt einfach loswerden. «Am I right?»

McGregor nickte zur Bestätigung. Er erzählte, wie er fünf Tage zuvor mittags Mr. Lorrington, den ‹verdächtigen› Buchhalter der United Chemicals, mit dem Stand der Ermittlungen konfrontiert hatte.

«He was very nervous, as you can imagine. I told him that he would make things a lot easier for himself if he cooperated.

If he gave us the information we needed, we might not even have to prosecute him. He told me to come out to his house in Ashford later that afternoon – that's out west, near Heathrow Airport. He said he would give me something there, a disk with relevant data. Maybe I shouldn't have let him go, but it seemed to be the best way to get results at the time. After all those months it was finally beginning to look promising.»

Er fummelte wieder an seiner Pfeife herum. Kein Wunder, daß er niemanden fängt, dachte Florian. Wenn er so langsam ist, wie er erzählt, sind alle längst weg. Aber vielleicht redet er ja nur so langsam, damit Manni und ich als Nicht-Engländer auch alles mitbekommen, gestand er dem Inspektor zu. Also was war nun mit dem verdächtigen Buchhalter? Hatte er mit der Polizei zusammengearbeitet, um eine Anklage gegen sich zu vermeiden? Wenn er tatsächlich eine Diskette zusammengestellt hatte, dann war das wohl die, hinter der alle her waren.

«Inspector Yardley and I drove out to Ashford later that afternoon,» McGregor continued. «I got out of the car, went to the front door and rang the bell. No one answered. I walked around the house to the back. Through a window looking out onto the garden, I could see him lying on the floor. I broke open the door and ran over to him. He was dead alright. We later discovered that he had died as a result of a heart attack. Poor chap. The excitement was obviously too much for him. He lived alone, too. I was having a look around the place when Inspector Yardley radioed that a black Volvo was slowly approaching the house, that it was now parking about a hundred yards away. We knew already from our observation of United Chemicals that it was one of their company cars, used by the company's security department.»

Also waren die Spieße und der Mann mit dem Schnurrbart Werkschutzleute bei United Chemicals, dachte Manni, der in

Gedanken wieder vor sich sah, wie der Volvo vorgefahren kam und ihm nach King's Cross entwischte. Er konnte sich nicht vorstellen, was der tote Buchhalter mit der vertauschten Diskette zu tun hatte, als Toter konnte er dem Inspektor ja schlecht eine Diskette überreicht haben.

«It was one of those situations where you think of a thousand things in the space of one second, and act completely instinctively. We had just lost our one and only lead, and now these security people from United Chemicals had just turned up. Yardley radioed that two men had just got out of the car and were walking towards the house. Lorrington had been a relatively small fish, we knew that much, so someone higher up in the company must also have been involved – a big fish, so to speak. Maybe the security people could lead us to him, but how? To catch a big fish, we would need to find a big bait.»

Florian und Maddy sahen sich an und mußten lachen. Sie waren also nicht die einzigen Köder in diesem Spiel gewesen.

Das darf ja wohl nicht wahr sein, durchfuhr es Manni, dem die Situation plötzlich klar wurde. Dann hat der wahrscheinlich einfach irgendeine Diskette genommen und ist mit dieser Diskette rausgelaufen, spekulierte er. Und die Spieße sollten glauben, daß es die echte ist.

Manni hatte richtig kombiniert, denn McGregor fuhr fort:

«I decided that I would be the bait. Told Inspector Yardley my plan, well, made it up as I was talking to her over the radio, to be honest. She got out of the car, left the key in the ignition, I grabbed a small empty disk box from beside the computer, put a disk into it which was lying around, ran out of the front door with the box clearly visible in my hand, got into the car and drove off. Yardley walked to the next phone box and set everything up in Edinburgh. Just as I had hoped, the men from United Chemicals went straight back to the car and followed me to Heathrow Airport, where I bought a ticket for the shuttle to Edinburgh. They did likewise.»

Während Maddy fragte, warum denn gerade Edinburgh, fiel Manni auf, daß der Plan einige Lücken hatte. Klar, die Spieße, wie immer sie auch hießen, sollten denken, daß er eine Diskette mit wichtigen Informationen über die Betrüger hatte. Offensichtlich hatten die Betrüger am Nachmittag gemerkt, daß mit dem Buchhalter was nicht stimmte, sonst hätten sie die Spieße ja nicht hingeschickt. Vielleicht hatte er sich auffällig benommen, was Besonderes kopiert oder so. Soweit ok. Dann sollten die Werkschutz-Spieße also hinter dem Inspektor her, wahrscheinlich sollten sie die Diskette klauen und sie zu dem großen Fisch bringen. Und die Polizei sollte ihnen dabei auf der Spur bleiben. Nur, würden bei einer wahllos gegriffenen Diskette nicht sogar schon Werkschutzleute auf ihren Computern erkennen, daß da etwas nicht stimmte? Er und Maddy hatten beim ersten Blick auf das *Directory* schließlich schon gedacht, daß die Daten nicht gerade aufregend aussahen.

«Well, there were three reasons for Edinburgh, really,» McGregor explained, «one was that I wanted them to follow me far away from London, hopefully into territory which was unknown to them, so that it would be easier to follow their movements and trace them to the big fish.»

Ganz schön aufwendig für so einen Grund, dachte Florian. Auch McGregors zweiter Grund – nach Edinburgh gab es dauernd Flüge, so daß er nicht lange in ungeschützten öffentlichen Räumen warten mußte, überzeugte ihn nicht. Die sollten ihn doch angreifen, dachte er.

«But the most important reason was the disk. You see, I had just grabbed any old disk that was lying around. I wanted them to steal it from me and bring it to the big fish. But if they got the disk which I had taken, then they'd find out as soon as they got to the next computer, that there wasn't a single piece of information about them on it. So if the disk could be damaged somehow, and be seen to be damaged in a credible way, they wouldn't be able to do anything with it, but at the same time wouldn't know whether or not it was important. That way I hoped they would bring it to the big fish and one of his experts. And what more credible and visable way of damaging a disk than a spectacular hit-and-run car accident where the disk goes flying out of its box through the air and lands somewhere in the middle of a road? There was only one person who could drive a hit-and-run car the way I wanted it, and that was my old friend Douglas in Edinburgh.

Doch nicht so schlecht, mußte Florian anerkennen. Der hatte wirklich an alles gedacht.

Diesen Plan hätten ihm die Computer-Experten bestimmt nicht genehmigt, dachte Manni. Jeder weiß doch, daß eine Diskette ruhig durch die Luft fliegen kann, ohne daß dadurch die Daten unbedingt beschädigt werden. Magneten wären da eine bessere Lösung gewesen, aber wie veranstaltet man so etwas spektakulär in der Öffentlichkeit?

Der Inspektor lehnte sich zurück und sah einen Moment lang recht zufrieden aus. Dieser Teil des Plans hatte ihm wohl am besten gefallen.

«It wasn't a bad plan, even if I say so myself, for one that was thought out on the spur of the moment. Inspector Yardley got in touch with Edinburgh to set up the stunt, the men tracked me to the airport, got a ticket to Edinburgh, checked in just behind me, and everything was going well according to plan until you came on the scene.» He was looking at Maddy with a concerned expression on his face.

«In order to make a show, for the benefit of my pursuers, about how important the disk was, I had to kick up quite a fuss at the x-ray machine where the hand-luggage is checked.

I told the man that I was not going to have my data wiped out in it and insisted that he hand-searched it.»

Von wegen *kick up a fuss*, dachte Manni, das brauchteste gar nicht. Die Kontrolleure, die das Handgepäck überprüfen, akzeptieren es immer, wenn man die Disketten nicht röntgen lassen will und überprüfen sie per Hand, das ist Standard. Für jemand, der ein Computer-Verbrechen aufklären sollte, wußte McGregor erstaunlich wenig über die Technik, fand Manni.

Während er das dachte, hatte Maddy den Inspektor unterbrochen und ihm den Diskettentausch geschildert, so wie die vier ihn sich in Wimbledon ausgemalt hatten. Wimbledon. Ob er überhaupt noch ein Spiel würde sehen können? Schließlich mußte er am übernächsten Tag wieder zurückfliegen.

«And did it really happen that way?» Maddy wanted to know.

«Yes, unfortunately,» McGregor replied, «but who would ever have thought of it – it seemed so unlikely.»

«It wouldn't have happened if there were more business *women* in this country.» Das war das erste, was Florian Park, die nun Yardley hieß, sagen hörte. Prompt fing sie sich einen mißbilligenden Blick von Inspektor McGregor ein. Was sie wohl damit gemeint hatte? Ach ja, die Warteschlange fürs Abtasten – es waren so wenig Frauen dagewesen.

«You know the next part of the story already,» continued McGregor, «everything went according to plan in Edinburgh. We had a terrific accident, the box and the disk flew through the air, the ambulance arrived quickly, one of the men grabbed the disk, ran off with it, we tailed them, tapped all possible phones, the usual business, you know. But then things didn't quite work out the way we wanted them to.»

Als die Spieß-Gesellen Maddys Diskette in dem Computer hatten, müssen sie sich ganz schön veräppelt vorgekommen

sein, dachte Florian. Wer fliegt schon gern nach Edinburgh, bloß um mit ‹Dear Grandad› angeredet zu werden und Kopien von Computerspielen zu erhalten. Aber warum dachten die Spieße dann nicht einfach, daß das die Diskette von dem Detektiv war, der sie bloß in die Irre führen wollte? Warum sollten sie annehmen, daß ein Diskettentausch stattgefunden hatte? Es dauerte einige Zeit, bis Florian diesen Einwand auf englisch formuliert hatte.

«Yes,» Maddy supported him, «it shouldn't have made any difference whether it was your disk they got or mine, as long as they *thought* it was yours and saw that there was no incriminating evidence on it. Why should they suspect anything and go on searching?»

«Yes, we were wondering about that, too,» McGregor replied, «and found a possible explanation. Obviously the dead accountant, Lorrington, had actually done something that afternoon before he had the heart attack, so they were convinced that there *was* a genuine disk somewhere. While we were in the plane to Edinburgh, less than two hours after I had first set foot in Lorrington's house, someone else went in there – with a key – took all the floppy disks and wiped the hard disk clean. We didn't have a surveillance team there at the time – staff shortages, you know. The burglar obviously didn't find the disk he was looking for, so they were convinced that it had been taken by me. But it wasn't the one they found at the scene of the accident, so they had to keep on looking.»

Schon wieder ein Einbruch, bei dem nur eine Festplatte gelöscht wurde. Ob man als ‹Festplattenlöscheinbrecher› wohl eine Spezialausbildung braucht, dachte Florian. Muß ja ein öder Job sein – da kommt man in eine Wohnung voll mit Sachen, die man klauen könnte, und was macht man – drückt Knöpfe am Computer.

«Another thing which kept them going,» McGregor continued, «was that they, like you, figured out quite quickly how the disks could have been swapped at the airport – and that would explain why they had a birthday disk instead of the real one. You shouldn't underestimate them. Dennis Grade especially is a very clever man.»

Dennis Grade, so erfuhren Maddy, Florian und Manni, war der Mann mit dem Schnurrbart. Ein ehemaliger Polizist, der jetzt einen der höheren Posten im Werkschutz der United Chemicals bekleidete. Spieß hieß in Wirklichkeit Sanders und war von der Armee zu United Chemicals gegangen. Frau Spieß, wie sie sie nannten, war eine ehemalige Gefängnisaufseherin namens Briggs.

«So, instead of leading us to the big fish after they got the disk as we had hoped,» McGregor continued, «they led us to all kinds of people who were in that plane to Edinburgh. They obviously accessed the British Airways computer, and checked out the passengers. That marketing story was a clever trick.»

Nur bedingt, dachte Florian, wir jedenfalls fanden den Anruf gleich etwas komisch.

Manni hatte inzwischen gefragt, ob die Spieß-Gesellen denn nicht damit rechneten, daß die Diskette bei der Polizei auftauchen würde – wenn jemand per Zufall eine Diskette mit so wichtigen Daten finden würde, würde der dann nicht zur Polizei gehen? Ob das Grade nicht auffällig erschienen sei, daß das nicht passiert war?

McGregors Antwort bestand im wesentlichen aus einem Achselzucken. Damit mußten er und Yardley rechnen, gestand er zu, aber was hätte man anderes machen können, als die Sache trotzdem auszuprobieren.

«We put that faked article about my death into the paper,» he continued, «to make them believe that the police hadn't got the disk.»

«And,» Inspector Yardley butted in, «at the same time we were wondering how three people with good records, now working for the security department of United Chemicals, could all have turned criminal. Maybe they didn't really know what was going on, maybe the big fish had fooled them by telling them a story – that foreign spies were after a United Chemicals secret formula or something like that. We thought if they read about a case of computer fraud, they might come to the police themselves.»

«But they didn't,» Maddy concluded. Yardley nodded.

Gute Idee mit dem gefälschten Artikel, mußte Florian anerkennen. Denn irgendwie war es ja schon komisch, daß drei ehemalige Beamte plötzlich Komplizen von Betrügern geworden waren.

«So they finally found you, Maddy, and broke into your house,» Yardley went on, «and that really worried us. When children are involved the picture changes completely. We wanted to call the whole thing off straight away.»

Wir sind doch keine Kinder, dachte Florian ärgerlich. «Why didn't you, then?» fragte er vorwurfsvoll, denn er sah, wie bleich Maddy geworden war. Auch ihr war erst Schritt für Schritt klar geworden, in was für einer Gefahr sie sich befunden hatte.

«Well, we should have, but we thought after the break-in at the Butler's that that was it and Maddy would be taken off their list. We didn't know that you were, in fact, the disk swapper. So when you came to the police station that evening with the container to be fingerprinted, Constable Wright had orders to tell you that it wasn't at all suspicious and to go home like a good girl. We thought they were finished with you and would go on looking somewhere else.»

«What we didn't expect,» here Inspector Yardley took up the story, «was that they would stay on your track and keep trying. We only realized that after Sanders stole your handbag at Wimbledon and Briggs brought it back to the lost property office. They were so careful not to let you suspect that they were after something.»

Aber die hatten nicht mit uns gerechnet, dachte Manni, nicht damit, daß wir sie in Wimbledon beschatten würden.

«After that we decided to concentrate all our efforts on watching them and you,» continued Yardley, «but you can believe me that we didn't feel very good about it.»

Das ist ja Wahnsinn, dachte Florian, die Polizei wußte die ganze Zeit, daß Maddy in Gefahr war, und hat sie trotzdem einfach als Köder benutzt. Dürfen sie das? Ihr eigenes Köder-Spiel kam ihm plötzlich sehr albern vor. *Zentrale an Köder* – von wegen! Sie waren alle Köder gewesen.

«The trouble was that you made yourself look even more suspicious by playing that silly Cops and Robbers game, following them about and setting false traps. That really convinced them that you knew something,» McGregor said.

Florian und Manni protestierten heftig. Von wegen Räuber und Gendarm. Irgendwie mußten sie doch die Spieße von Maddy ablenken und versuchen herauszufinden, wer hinter ihnen her war und warum. Schließlich hatte die Polizei es ja abgelehnt, Maddy zuzuhören.

«Alright, alright,» Inspector Yardley calmed them down, «maybe it was ok from your point of view. But they saw what you were up to straight away and decided to seperate you. You should have heard the telephone conversation that Sanders and Briggs had after she had got into her car and Sanders had arrived at United Chemicals. She had a good laugh about Grade following Maddy following her.»

Florian wäre am liebsten im Erdboden versunken. Zentrale, dein Plan war doch wohl nicht so brillant, mußte er sich eingestehen.

Auch Manni fühlte sich nicht besonders großartig. Spieß, oder Sanders, wie er jetzt wohl hieß, hatte ihn sogar extra veräppelt, als er ihm beim Fahrkartenkauf einen deutschen Akzent vorgespielt hatte. Von wegen den Spieß umdrehen. Die Spieße hatten sie ganz schön umgedreht.

Moment mal, dachte Florian plötzlich, da Park nicht zu denen gehörte, warum hatte sie dann Sakina abgeschüttelt?

Yardley laughed when Florian asked her about it. «Believe it or not, I didn't even see her tailing me. She must have been the only successful shadow in the whole operation. It was a pure coincidence that she hopped into the express bus. Jimmy had taken over watch in the car and I just went home. Not for long, as it happened – when we heard you and Maddy on the phone deciding to go to King's Cross, I had to go there straight away, too.»

«You tapped our phone as well,» Maddy shouted, «that's awful!»

«Yes it is awful,» admitted Inspector McGregor, «but then so is everything else. The fact that they attacked you at King's Cross is awful, too, and we shouldn't have let it happen.»

«Wenn du nicht von 'ner Telefonzelle in Wimbledon aus in Edinburgh angerufen hättest, sondern von zu Hause aus, dann hätte die Polizei durch das Abhören eures Telefons sogar noch eher gewußt, daß die Diskette in King's Cross ankommt», sagte Florian zu Maddy.

She nodded, but her thoughts were elsewhere. She was still furious that their phone was tapped. Who had she phoned over the past three days and what had she said?

Florian sagte dann der Polizei, daß sie ihnen in King's Cross doch sehr geschickt zu Hilfe gekommen seien.

«Thanks, Florian,» said Yardley, but she didn't look totally happy, «I thought it was all a bit too obvious. Still, it was a good try.»

McGregor sighed. «I suppose we blew the whole thing, really. All we can do now is to take your statements, inform your parents about what's been happening and apologize to them. Then we'll arrest the trio. It would be nice if they would tell us something about the big fish, but very unlikely. It's not much, is it? We could have arrested them days ago. All that work for nothing.»

Er sah ziemlich niedergeschlagen aus. Kann nicht leicht für ihn sein, dachte Florian mitleidig, so viel Einsatz und jetzt muß er den großen Fisch doch von der Angel lassen. Einige Augenblicke saßen alle etwas ratlos herum. Then Maddy got up.

«They don't necessarily know that we are here now, do they?» she asked slowly. «What if I have looked at the information on my computer and, rather than going to the police, I've decided to get in touch with the big fish to do a deal with United Chemicals?»

Chapter Twelve

in which there are plenty of secret phone calls und in dem der große Fisch sich zu einem Treffen bereit erklärt

Es dauerte einige Zeit, bis Florian, Maddy, Manni und die Polizisten Maddys Idee durchdiskutiert und zu einem Plan verarbeitet hatten.

Maddy was frustrated and her enthusiasm dampened by all the Inspectors' *ifs* and *buts* and by the number of times they said ‹you don't really think that professional criminals of their intelligence would fall for that, do you?›, and ‹I don't think someone of your age would be taken seriously in such a situation›.

Florian war nach zwei Stunden total erschöpft. Was für ein Tag! Erst war er völlig nutzlos als Köder durch die Gegend gelaufen, dann hatte er erfahren, wie schlecht man sich fühlt, wenn jemand einem die Luft abklemmt, und nun hatte er einer erhitzten Diskussion auf englisch folgen müssen, in der es nur so von langen *‹if… then, but…›* Sätzen wimmelte. Er selber hatte wenig gesagt, aber das lag nicht so sehr daran, daß auf englisch geredet wurde. Sein Plan, Spieß und Co zu verfolgen, war so schiefgegangen, daß er sich nicht traute, überhaupt noch irgend etwas vorzuschlagen.

In the end even Maddy had to admit that the plan they had all worked out was fine. Her only complaint was that it had taken so long. Now came the not so nice part, where the police would have to talk to their parents.

Sakinas und Maddys Eltern fielen aus allen Wolken, als sie von den Ereignissen der letzten Tage erfuhren, während Herr Hutzner erstaunlich gelassen blieb. Florians Eltern waren auf ihrer Safari nicht zu erreichen. Gott sei dank, dachte Florian nur, seine Mutter wäre glatt imstande gewesen, Löwen Löwen sein zu lassen und nach London zu fliegen. Überhaupt gefiel ihm die neue Richtung nicht. Was am Morgen ein riesiger Spaß für ihn gewesen war, war plötzlich ernst. In Abwesenheit seiner Eltern übernahm Mr. Butler die, wie er es nannte, *responsibility for Florian*.

After thinking long and hard about it, and after giving out harshly to their daughter about her involvement in the whole thing, finally even Sakina's parents agreed to the plan. Now it could proceed.

Florian und Maddy zogen mit in das Haus von Inspektor Yardley ein, das Butlersche Haus wurde gut bewacht, Sakinas Eltern erzählten jedem, daß ihre Tochter Hausarrest habe. Sie dürfe nicht aus dem Haus, weil sie ohne ihre Erlaubnis nach Wimbledon gegangen sei.

Manni sollte mit seinem Vater am nächsten Tag nach Wimbledon gehen, so wie es ja eigentlich die ganze Zeit geplant war. Zu seiner Sicherheit wurde ein Beamter in Zivil abgestellt. Toller Job, dachte Manni, auf mich aufpassen und dabei ein Halbfinale sehen.

«Do we really need protection?» hatte er gefragt.

«It's just a precaution», hatte McGregor geantwortet, «if the people at United Chemicals can be convinced that Maddy still has the disk and hasn't contacted the police, then they might just try to grab one of her friends so that they'd have something to trade for it. But I don't think they will. These are very smart people we are dealing with, I don't think they will stoop to using old-fashioned methods like kidnapping or shooting their way out of things. But we can never be too sure.»

The following morning an electronic message appeared on Dennis Grade's screen after he switched on his computer.

```
Message from:
Maddy Butler

to:
Dennis Grade (name provided courtesy of the late Mr.
Lorrington)


re: interest in a computer/business job


As a result of certain information obtained from Mr.
Lorrington, I feel encouraged to ask for an appointment
with a high-ranking representative of your company. I
would like to explore the possibilities of my entering
the firm/club, offering my computer expertise to
cooperate in the line of business indicated by Mr.
Lorrington.

I shall phone you at 11.11 a.m. sharp.
```

The police computer experts had broken into the United Chemicals' network and had sent that message to Grade's electronic mailbox. But Maddy had insisted on writing the message herself.

Trotz der bequemen Couch in Frau Yardleys Wohnzimmer war Florian an diesem Morgen schon sehr früh aufgewacht. Er war aufgeregt, obwohl er eigentlich keine große Rolle zu spielen hatte. Auch Maddy kam schon sehr früh aus Inspektor Yardleys Gästezimmer. Sie saßen herum, frühstückten kaum und verbrachten die Zeit bis elf Uhr damit, irgendwas im Fernsehen anzuschauen, was sie sofort wieder vergaßen.

«Ready?» Yardley finally asked.
Maddy nodded.
«And remember, you want to talk to the big fish.»
Maddy nodded again.
Florian versuchte, die Beine auszustrecken, aber einen Augenblick später saß er schon wieder mit fest angewinkelten und angespannten Beinen in seinem Sessel. Maddy hatte jetzt den Hörer in der Hand und tippte die Zahlen ein, Inspektor Yardley hatte das Mithörgerät am Ohr.
«United Chemicals, good morning, can I help you?»
«Mr. Grade from Security, please», Maddy tried to sound firm.
»Just one moment please.»
Maddy could hear some clicking noises.
«Hello, Grade here.»
«This is Maddy Butler. Did you get my message?»
«Yes.»
«Well?»
«Well what?»
«Are you interested in the disk?»
«Maybe.»
«Then I would like to speak to whoever told you to get it from me.»
«I'm afraid that won't be possible.»
«I'm afraid it will have to be possible. I'll phone again at 11.44 sharp.» Maddy put down the phone.
Alle Achtung, dachte Florian, das klang gut. Echt ruhig. Dabei lief ihr der Schweiß von der Stirn.
The next half-hour crawled by. Then Maddy phoned again, and got put through to Grade's extension.
«Grade here.»
«It's Maddy again.»
«Yes.» There was a short pause.

«Well, can I speak to...»

«Not now over the phone.»

Florian sah, wie Maddy und Yardley siegreich lächelten. Also hat Teil 1 geklappt, dachte er erleichtert, der Mann muß ein Treffen vorgeschlagen haben.

«Ok, somewhere else then,» said Maddy lightly, «I'm easy.»

«The person concerned isn't in at the moment. Maybe we could phone you later to arrange something.»

Inspector Yardley raised her forefinger in warning to Maddy but that wasn't necessary. Maddy had an answer ready.

«I wasn't born yesterday, you know, even though you seem to think so. I've left home so that you can't find me. You don't think I'm going to give you my new number just like that, do you? I could suggest a meeting-place, though.»

Gut, daß wir das vorher alles geübt hatten, dachte Florian, der Frau Yardleys Geste und Maddys Antwort entnehmen konnte, daß das Gespräch inzwischen beim Thema Treffpunkt angekommen war. Schade, daß er nicht auch so einen Mithöranschluß hatte.

Grade laughed. «All in good time, young lady, hold your horses. When do you think *we* were born? Ok, you ring us again at 12.12, twelve minutes past noon, and we'll tell you where you can meet him.»

Him – a man, Maddy thought. Florian hatte vor lauter Aufregung schon das zweite Yorkie, einen Schokoladenriegel, in Angriff genommen.

Der dritte Anlauf war kurz und sachlich gewesen. Grade hatte gesagt, Maddy solle in eine Telefonzelle gehen und von dort aus in fünfzehn Minuten wieder anrufen und die Telefonnummer der Zelle durchsagen. ‹Er› würde sie dann kurz von einer anderen Zelle aus anrufen. Er würde sich als der *Juggler* melden.

Geht das denn so einfach, hatte Florian gefragt, in Deutschland kann man überhaupt nur in ganz wenigen Zellen angerufen werden. Es geht, bestätigte ihm Maddy, «if the phone isn't out of order». Then she turned to Inspector Yardley. «If I tell them the number of the phone, won't his people be able to find us there?» she asked.

«Not that quickly,» answered Yardley, «and anyway, we'll drive you to a phone box outside West Norwood, a rather special one.» She smiled.

Florian wollte wissen, was er denn nun tun konnte. Die Inspektorin erklärte ihm, daß er erst mal nur in der Wohnung bleiben und warten müßte. Per Telefon gab sie Anweisung, jeden zu fotografieren, der in der nächsten halben Stunde aus dem Gebäude der United Chemicals in eine der umliegenden Telefonzellen ging. Außerdem ordnete sie an, daß alle Anrufe in der *special box* zu ihrem Ausgangspunkt zurückverfolgt werden sollten.

Inspector Yardley and Maddy drove from West Norwood to Brixton. «Oh no», said Maddy when they got there, «someone is in the telephone box. And it's just over fifteen minutes now since the last phone call.»

That someone got out of the box as soon as they arrived there and held the door open for Maddy. «It's all yours, madam», said Jimmy with a smile.

Maddy phoned Grade, gave the number of her phone and waited. A minute later the phone rang.

«Hello, is that Maddy?» said a very charming voice.

«Yes,» she managed to say.

«The juggler here. Look, I'm sorry about this silly game of hide and seek. It's not really my sort of thing. I like to do straight business. But we have reason to believe that you have been to the police and that our phones at United Chemicals are being tapped.»

«But I didn't go to the police,» Maddy protested, «I was fascinated by the way you managed to manoeuvre all that money around. I want to be part of it. I want to be rich.»

Florian lief unruhig in der Wohnung hin und her. Wenn das nur gut geht, wenn das nur gut geht, dachte er. Der Plan hatte seiner Meinung nach zwei schwache Stellen. Der Juggler mußte Maddy glauben, daß sie die Diskette tatsächlich hatte. Na gut, der wußte selber nicht, was der Buchhalter alles aufgeschrieben hatte, insofern konnte Maddy mit den Informationen, die die Polizei schon hatte, bluffen. Aber das andere: wie konnte auch nur irgend jemand glauben, daß es Maddys Berufswunsch war, Computerbetrüger zu werden, und daß sie nur schnell reich werden wollte? Überraschenderweise hatten ihn McGregor und Yardley da beruhigt. London ist anders als du das aus deinen Schulbüchern kennst, hatten sie ihm gesagt, die älteren Herren mit Bowler und Regenschirm, die ihre Zeit in den Clubs verbringen und aus adligen Häusern stammen, gibt es kaum noch. Jetzt ist man sozialer Aufsteiger, verdient mit zweiundzwanzig riesige Gehälter, handelt mit Geld statt mit Waren, fährt Porsche, trinkt literweise Champagner, hat keine Moral und nur Interesse daran, mehr Geld zu machen.

«Bloody Yuppies», hatte McGregor am Schluß gesagt, «they are ruining everything that was good about good old England. They caught someone your age recently making huge sums of money speculating in stocks and shares. At your age! Did everything over the phone putting on a deep voice. And they would never have found out a thing about it if he hadn't lost money during the Crash last October. That's Thatcher's England for you – the enterprise culture.»

Offensichtlich hatte McGregor was gegen Yuppies. Florian dagegen fand Porsche und Champagner ganz gut. Hoffentlich ist der *Juggler* so 'n einseitiger Yuppie, der denkt, daß jeder nur reich werden will, dachte Florian, sonst kommt Maddy in irre Schwierigkeiten.

After the juggler had said that a girl who wanted to be rich was a girl after his own heart, he said: «You know that we will have to have a look at your disk, don't you?»

«Of course,» Maddy replied, «but I do have other copies of it stored in safe places.»

«That's what I would expect of a clever girl like you,» said the juggler in a flattering tone, «but I assume there are no funny letters to friends involved this time.»

Maddy blushed. «That was a stupid idea of Florian's,» she said. «But look, apart from all that, the police are bound to track me down at some stage, so I have a suggestion to make. Florian and I will meet you somewhere. I'll give you a copy of the disk you are after, so that you can see that I do have the real thing, and you give me a disk with data which looks like the real thing, except that it is filled with the wrong names, dates and figures. I will then go to the police with that disk – or even better, your heavies attack me, the police rescue me, your men manage to get away and the police find the disk on me, think it's the real one, and arrest the wrong people.»

«A wicked plan, Maddy, almost too clever to have been thought out by you.»

Maddy held her breath. Did he suspect something?

«But then, I sold my first computer program when I was fifteen,» he continued. «Geniuses just have to recognize other geniuses. I'd be delighted to introduce you to the business.»

Maddy was relieved. The juggler paused for a moment. «But it will take a while to make up the fake disk,» he said.

«Let me see, do you know Westminster pier – where the boats leave for Greenwich and the Thames Barrier?»

«Yes.»

«Be there at eleven o'clock tomorrow morning. Buy a ticket to Greenwich but don't get on to any of the boats. You'll be told what to do.»

He hung up.

«Der hat das also geglaubt», freute sich Florian, nachdem ihm Maddy alles haarklein berichtet hatte. Sie konnte das Telefongespräch fast Wort für Wort wiedergeben, so konzentriert war sie offensichtlich gewesen. Inspektor Yardley hatte inzwischen erfahren, daß niemand von United Chemicals aus in eine Telefonzelle gegangen war, sondern daß der Anruf von einer Zelle in den Docklands gekommen war.

«Clever fellow,» she said, «so he was obviously in a public phone box already. Grade phoned him there and told him your number. So he couldn't be traced to the firm or be seen leaving it to go to a phone box. Very clever indeed.»

Die Docklands, so hatte sie Florian erklärt, das sei bis vor kurzem ein heruntergekommenes, kaum noch genutztes Hafenviertel gewesen, das nun mit riesigem Aufwand in ein reiches Wohn- und Industriegebiet verwandelt worden war. Tolle Häuser am Wasser mit eigener Bootsanlegestelle gebe es dort, wenn man es sich leisten könne.

«Well», war Yardley fortgefahren, «Westminster pier and Docklands. Interesting. Can you swim?»

Dreizehntes Kapitel

das leer bleibt, weil die Dreizehn für Florian und Maddy Unglück bringen könnte

Chapter Fourteen

about which nothing will be told in advance

That whole evening was spent on the telephone. Maddy told Sakina what had happened – und Florian bestand darauf, auch ein bißchen mit ihr zu plaudern. Dann berichtete Florian Manni, was gelaufen war. Manni hatte zwar Steffi Graf und Pam Shriver spielen gesehen, aber so richtig bei der Sache war er nicht gewesen, sondern in Gedanken bei Maddy und Florian.

«Und morgen früh geht's zurück», sagte er, «Berlin via Hamburg. Ich wäre ja echt lieber mit euch am Pier.»

Maddy phoned Janet, too, to tell her the latest news. Janet said that her interview had gone well; she would hear from them in about four day's time.

Maddy and Florian hardly slept a wink that night and were up very early. Yardley and McGregor had everything organized. Every excursion boat leaving Westminster pier for Greenwich or the Thames Barrier from half past ten onwards would have plain clothes detectives on it, police ‹tourists› were hanging around on Westminster bridge and near the pier, and the police boats at the Waterloo bridge pier were on alert.

«Wir reden deutsch, wenn was ist», sagte Florian zu Maddy, «vielleicht versteht der Juggler das nicht.»

«Ok,» Maddy nodded. She had tried to create a few files on a disk which looked as if they contained some secret information, but she knew that the juggler would see through it straight away.

Florian versuchte, sie in diesem Punkt zu beruhigen. «Sieh

mal», sagte er, «der denkt ja, ihr tauscht bloß die Disketten. Und bevor er an seinem Computer ist und sie sich ansieht, hat ihn die Polizei schon erwischt. Er glaubt doch, daß die Polizei erst später bei der gespielten Übergabe auftauchen wird.»

«That's only if he believed me.» Maddy wasn't too sure.

Yardley was on the phone to the police computer experts. «Any results from the surveillance of United Chemicals' computers yet?» she asked.

«No, but it won't be long now,» she received in reply.

McGregor übernahm die Einsatzleitung, die bei der Wasserschutzpolizei an der Waterloo Bridge Quartier bezog. Yardley fuhr zu den Computerspezialisten ins Präsidium.

Kurz vor elf standen Florian und Maddy am Pier. Als von Big Ben das 11-Uhr-Läuten herübertönte, zuckte Florian zusammen. In Fernsehfilmen, die in London spielen, hört man immer Big Ben, bevor etwas Schreckliches passiert. Aber da ist dann meist auch Nebel, tröstete er sich und blinzelte in die Sonne.

Boats arrived, boarded their passengers and left again. Big Ben struck the quarter hour. Maddy wandered up and down. No one had told them what to do yet.

Florian sah sich um. Keiner der Touristen sah aus wie ein Polizist. So beschattet man also richtig, dachte er beschämt. Er hatte das Scheitern seines Plans immer noch nicht ganz verdaut.

Big Ben struck the half hour. Maddy was becoming extremely tense. Still no sign of anyone. Had the juggler just made fun of her? Did he know that it was a police trap? Had he played along so that the police would concentrate their efforts here while he just slipped out of the country?

«Pan Am regrets to announce that due to a late incoming flight and restrictions by air traffic control, flight number PA 102 to Hamburg and Berlin, scheduled for 10.25, will be delayed by approximately three hours. Eine Durchsage für Passagiere gebucht auf den Pan Am Flug Nummer 102 nach Hamburg und Berlin um 10.25. Aufgrund der verspäteten Ankunft der Maschine aus Berlin und der Beschränkungen durch die Flugüberwachung wird sich der Abflug voraussichtlich um etwa drei Stunden verzögern», kam es über den Lautsprecher im Wartebereich des Terminals 3 auf dem Flughafen Heathrow.

«O nein», schimpfte Manni, «das darf doch nicht wahr sein. Dafür mußten wir so früh aufstehen und uns in die *rush hour*-U-Bahn quetschen. Und was machen wir jetzt?» fragte er seinen Vater.

«Abwarten und Tee trinken», sagte Herr Hutzner und vertiefte sich in seine Zeitung.

One boat after the next had come and gone, and Maddy and Florian were left waiting on the pier. Should they give up and go home? Had McGregor been right when he had said that there was only an outside chance that the plan might work? Big Ben struck a quarter to twelve.

A young man in a leather jacket and tie who had been waiting on the pier for a while approached them. «Hello, you two. Sorry about the delay, but I had to make sure that there weren't any more of you than you said there would be. Our excursion party should be a small one,» he smiled at them.

Praktisch aus dem Nichts war während seiner Worte ein schnittiges Motorboot herangefahren, mit Spieß – oder Sanders, wie er wohl richtig hieß – am Steuer und dem Mann mit dem Schnurrbart, Grade, daneben. In Windeseile waren Florian und Maddy im Boot, gestoßen vom Juggler, gezogen von Grade und aus eigenem Antrieb.

The boat took off at a great speed down the Thames. In no time at all it passed by Waterloo bridge where the police boats were docked.

Keines der Boote schien Anstalten zu machen, ihnen nachzujagen; bei dem Tempo hätten sie es wohl auch kaum geschafft. Hoffentlich hat die Polizei unseren Abgang mitgekriegt, dachte Florian, und hoffentlich fällt ihnen was ein.

«Welcome on board the cleverest computer financial transaction in history,» lachte der Juggler, während das Boot auf die Tower Bridge zuschoß. Er schlug die Decke, die einen Gegenstand auf der hinteren Bank verdeckte, zurück.

Maddy went pale. Oh God no, she thought, he's brought along a portable computer.

«Now let's have a look at what my old friend Mr. Lorrington managed to reveal. It's a pity about him, really. He was typical of the old brigade, didn't want to play along in the beginning – can you imagine not wanting to make a couple of megabucks on the side? – but I needed him to get our little transaction off the ground. Clever transaction, brilliant networking, people involved from twelve institutions in six countries. Easy as pie once you know how it works. Poor old Lorrington. He didn't want to join in our game. Fancied himself as a gentleman of the old school. So I had to make him join. He didn't want it to be known that he was gay – he had kept it a secret all his life. Stupid, isn't it?» He smiled again, but the smile had become less friendly, more eerie and sinister.

«Ok, let's get down to business and have a look at the disk, shall we. It *is* Lorrington's disk, isn't it?»

Florian sah, wie Maddy zitterte. Der Juggler hatte den Computer eingeschaltet und verlangte nach der Diskette. Maddy didn't know what to do. She opened her handbag very slowly. Why couldn't someone have stolen my bag today, she thought.

Wie kann ich ihr helfen, fragte sich Florian. Wie kann ich ihr bloß helfen? Das Boot jagte gerade mit voller Geschwindigkeit an der Anlegestelle Greenwich vorbei. Maddy hatte die Diskette jetzt in der Hand und reichte sie rüber.

«Ej, guck mal da, der tolle Park», schrie Florian gegen den Motorenlärm an und stieß beim Zeigen so gegen Maddy, daß ihr Arm über die Bordwand reichte.

Maddy dropped the disk into the water.

Das irre Lächeln des Jugglers wurde zu einem bösartigen Grinsen. «You little bastard», rief er und schlug Florian mit dem Handrücken ins Gesicht, «so it was a trap after all.» Er wandte sich an Grade: «You take care of them in the old warehouse», befahl er.

Nach vorn zu Sanders, der das Boot mit unverminderter Geschwindigkeit vorwärtsjagte, schrie er: «Drop me at the City airport.»

«Ich rufe noch mal bei Maddy zu Hause an», informierte Manni seinen Vater, «vielleicht sind sie ja jetzt zurück.»

Herr Hutzner nickte nur. Es war das vierte Mal, seit sie in den Warteraum für den Flug nach Hamburg / Berlin gegangen waren, daß sein Sohn versuchte anzurufen.

Manni ging zu den offenen Telefonen und wählte Maddys Nummer. Es läutete und läutete. Er sah sich um. Am Telefon neben seinem stand jetzt eine Frau im Nadelstreifenkostüm. Er legte den Hörer auf. Noch keiner da. Dann würde er den Rest eben in Berlin erfahren. Im Vorbeigehen hörte er die Frau am Nachbartelefon mit leicht erregter Stimme sagen: «He still hasn't got the disk back? Why not? It's only a bunch of kids he's dealing with, for God's sake. He gave us his word at the meeting...» Der Rest ging in der Lautsprecheransage unter:

«Pan Am Flight 102 to Hamburg and Berlin is now ready for boarding at gate 10. Pan Am Flug 102 nach...»

«Komm, Manni, es geht endlich los, auf zu Reihe 5 Sitz D und E», sagte Herr Hutzner.

How do we get out of this one, thought Maddy in desperation, what the hell do we do now? The juggler was gone. Sanders had raced along to the pier of the new City airport which could be reached by boat and the juggler had got out. Now they were left there, sitting opposite Grade who was holding an extremely sharp-looking knife pointed in their direction. Sanders was driving more slowly since they had left the airport and turned back, steering the boat into the water around the new buildings and old warehouses of the now fashionable Docklands.

Florian sah keinen Ausweg. Der Boss war weg, von der Polizei keine Spur, und die beiden sogenannten Werkschutzleute hatten sicher den Auftrag, ihn und Maddy zu beseitigen.

«What's going to happen to them?» hörte er Sanders Grade fragen. Er erhielt keine Antwort. «So, it was computer fraud and not a secret formula stolen by Worldwide Chemicals, as you tried to make Briggs and me believe. We've been covering up for a criminal all the time, have we?» ließ er nicht locker und nahm das Tempo runter.

«Shut up, Sanders», antwortete Grade, «you shouldn't worry your head about the details. You'll be getting an extra bonus for this case.»

«I'm not going to behave like a criminal», redete sich Sanders in Rage. «Trying to trace a stolen formula for the company using slightly illegal means is one thing, kidnapping children and covering up a computer fraud is another.»

Grade ging zu ihm hinüber. «Just keep driving», befahl er ihm und kam mit dem Messer bedrohlich nahe an seinen Hals. Sanders schlug es ihm aus der Hand und warf sich auf ihn. Beide fielen zu Boden und droschen aufeinander ein.

One of them must have fallen against the accelerator because all of a sudden the boat shot forward, at a great speed, towards the embankment.
«Jump!» Maddy screamed as she threw herself overboard into the cold, dirty water. Florian sprang hinterher.

Manni kam ins Schwitzen. Das lag nicht nur daran, daß ihn der Start des Flugzeugs nervös machte. Das auch. Aber mehr noch verwirrte ihn, was er soeben gehört und gesehen hatte. *Disk back*, *bunch of kids*, die Nadelstreifen – ein bißchen viel für eine zufällige Übereinstimmung, dachte er sich. Schade, daß er sich nicht mehr so genau an das Gesicht der Frau, die in Wimbledon in das *hospitality tent* der United Chemicals gegangen war, erinnern konnte. War sie die Frau, die gerade telefoniert hatte?

«Ladies and gentlemen, you may smoke now if you wish, but only in rows three and four in the Clipper class and in rows twenty to twenty-eight in...» kam es aus dem Lautsprecher, während die Boeing 727 durch den Watteteppich aus Wolken stieg. Dann das Ganze noch mal in akzentfreiem Deutsch. Und wenn ich mich total blamiere, dachte Manni, ich muß es riskieren.

Zwei Reihen vor ihm in der Clipper-Class, wo ihr gerade ein großes Frühstück serviert wurde, zündete die Frau im Nadelstreifenkostüm sich nervös eine Zigarette an.

«Uaaagh, about time too», said Maddy to the men from one of the police boats when they fished her out of the water. A second police boat picked up Sanders and Grade who had jumped out of their boat a few seconds after Maddy's and Florian's departure. All that could be seen of the boat was a huge ball of fire. It had exploded after crashing into the embankment wall.

Florian wurde kurz nach Maddy ebenfalls aus dem Wasser gezogen. Er schüttelte sich. «Dann lieber Sprachschule.»

In spite of everything, Maddy had to laugh. «But you were always complaining how boring your *Sprachschule* was and wanted to be on a classy boat instead», she said.

The policemen wrapped them up in blankets. «Back to Waterloo base,» said one of them. «McGregor won't be too happy with the results.» Nor am I, thought Maddy. If you tail high speed criminals you need high speed reactions and high speed boats. At least Florian, Manni, Sakina and she weren't the only ones to make fools of themselves during a chase.

Als die Stewardeß die Plastikbehälter mit dem bescheidenen Frühstück der *Economy class* abräumte, gab Manni ihr einen gefalteten Zettel mit der Aufschrift:

AN DIE BESATZUNG – DRINGEND – BITTE SOFORT LESEN (ABER SO, DASS DIE PASSAGIERE DAS NICHT BEMERKEN)

Die Stewardeß stutzte einen Augenblick, lächelte und ließ den Zettel in der Tasche ihrer Schürze verschwinden. Erschöpft lehnte sich Manni zurück. Er hatte aus allen Windungen seines Gehirns sein bestes Vorzeigedeutsch hervorgekramt und geschrieben:

Sehr geehrte Stewardeß, sehr geehrter Kapitän. Sicher denken Sie, dies ist ein Dummerjungenstreich. Oder Sie sagen, der hat zuviel Fernsehen gesehen. Beides stimmt aber nicht. Ich war in den letzten zwei Tagen bei der Aufklärung eines Falles von Großbetrug in London dabei. Funken Sie bitte nach London durch – an Inspector McGregor von Scotland Yard – daß höchstwahrscheinlich eine der Beteiligten, die Frau im Nadelstreifenkostüm auf Sitz 3A, in diesem Flugzeug nach Hamburg sitzt. Vielen Dank. Ihr Manfred Hutzner (Passagier nach Berlin, Sitz 5D).

Aus dem Lautsprecher tönte es:

«Ladies and gentlemen, this is the captain speaking. We are cruising at an altitude of 30000 feet. We will be landing in Hamburg in approximately twenty minutes. My apologies again for the delay. The weather in Hamburg is...»

Manni schloß die Augen. Ob Maddy und Florian alles gut überstanden hatten?

When the boat reached the police pier at Waterloo, a concerned looking McGregor was standing there waiting. «I am awfully sorry about this», he said as he helped them out of the boat, «we should never have let it happen. You'd better get out of those wet clothes quickly, we have dry ones inside for you.»

Florian nieste. «God bless», sagte McGregor. Gott sollte lieber die Polizei mit größerer Reaktionsfähigkeit segnen als mich und mein Niesen, dachte Florian.

Nachdem Maddy und Florian sich umgezogen hatten, fuhr McGregor zu Scotland Yard, wo Inspektor Yardley sie in einem Raum voller Computer erwartete. Maddy's eyes lit up.

«Wow!» she exclaimed. «Maybe I should try to blackmail *you* into letting me join your club.»

«This is the type of equipment we need in order to come to terms with the new breed of criminals,» said McGregor with a depressed expression on his face, «proper surveillance work, car stunts, phone tapping, chases – non of our traditional methods seem to work with computer crooks.»

Florian nieste. Ihn wunderte, daß Frau Yardley im Gegensatz zu McGregor gutgelaunt zu sein schien.

«Cheer up», sagte sie, «we've got him.»

«What – was!!» riefen McGregor, Maddy und Florian gleichzeitig.

«Yes, at the City airport.»

«So the computer surveillance was successful», sagte McGregor. Florian und Maddy verstanden nichts.

«You see», wandte sich Yardley ihnen zu, «when you told the juggler that you wanted to swap your disk for one with similar but wrong data, we knew that he would have to get a certain type of information out of United Chemicals' central computer. So, with the help of the president of the company and the head of computing, both of whom were very distressed at the idea of a major fraud operating from within United Chemicals, we recorded every access to the files which contained that information.»

Florian nieste. Das war ihm alles viel zu kompliziert. Also konnte man nicht nur Telefone überwachen, sondern auch Computer. Ein Computer konnte sich merken, wer was in ihm benutzt hatte! Erstaunlich, dachte er. Frau Yardley war inzwischen fortgefahren. Nur eine Person hatte auf fast alle in Frage kommenden Informationen zugegriffen – Patrick Lodge, Devisenabteilung. Das mußte der *Juggler* sein.

«We received that bit of information shortly after the two of you had jumped or were pushed onto his boat and we lost track of you.» Sie warf McGregor einen mißbilligenden Blick zu. «The rest was easy as pie. We called up his personal data, found out that he owned a private plane based at the City airport, sent a car out there immediately and had him arrested.»

«You have that kind of information about him in your computer?» asked Maddy amazed.

«We have that kind of information about a lot of people,» Yardley replied proudly.

«In that case I don't think I'd want to join your club,» Maddy said and made a face, «to keep track of other people's private affairs is not my idea of what computers are there for.»

Yardley shrugged her shoulders. «If we hadn't had the information about the plane, we wouldn't have been able to arrest Lodge, would you have preferred that?»

Maddy said nothing.

Einige Stunden später saßen alle im Wohnzimmer der Butlers. Bei einer Tasse heißem Tee sprachen sie die Ereignisse der letzten Tage noch einmal durch, unterbrochen nur durch Florians ständiges Geniese. Für Maddys Eltern waren die Ereignisse immer noch unglaublich.

Inspector Yardley hatte mit einer guten Nachricht begonnen. Lodge hatte, als er merkte, daß es keinen Ausweg gab, sich als Kronzeuge zur Verfügung gestellt und den ganzen Ring auffliegen lassen.

«They give me the creeps, these people,» McGregor commented, «no sense of honour or loyalty towards their fellow criminals. Just pure greed and the desire to get away with it, at anyone's cost.»

«But this one won't get away with everything this time, even if he is a key witness,» said Yardley. «There's the abduction of Florian and Maddy to be dealt with, and Sanders and Briggs will be good witnesses. They believed the ‹secret formula› story that Grade had told them – for a bit too long as far as I'm concerned; you obviously don't ask too many questions if the money is good – but they seem to be genuinely sorry about the business with the children now.»

Wenn die uns bloß nicht dauernd *children* nennen würden, dachte Florian. Frau Yardley hatte das Geständnis von Lodge ziemlich kurz zusammengefaßt. Eine weltweit operierende Gruppe hatte durch Manipulationen am Computerprogramm fremdes Geld hin und her und schließlich auf gut getarnte Privatkonten in der Schweiz und auf den Bahamas verschoben. Lodge hatte die Namen aller Beteiligten genannt. Die deutsche Repräsentantin war sogar schon festgenommen worden.

«And do you know how?» Yardley asked, not expecting an answer. «Your friend Manni spotted her on the plane and told us about his suspicions. We asked the German police to keep an eye on her, and when we got her name from Lodge, she was arrested on the spot.»

Florian und Maddy wollten wissen, wieso Manni denn jemanden verdächtig finden konnte, wenn noch nicht einmal die Polizei bei seinem Abflug nach Berlin wußte, wer der Juggler und seine Komplizen waren. Yardley erzählte, was Manni erlebt hatte. Dann berichtete sie über die ‹Jahreshauptversammlung› der Betrügergruppe.

«You'll never guess where they met – it was very cleverly disguised. Lodge invited them all once a year, as business associates, to Wimbledon. They could mix and meet very nicely in the hospitality tent of United Chemicals there. You can imagine how shocked the president of United Chemicals was when we told him about it.»

The phone rang. «It's for one of the inspectors,» said Mrs. Butler. McGregor took it.

«Fine,» he said before he put down the receiver. «I have a surprise for you,» he said smiling at Florian and Maddy, «that was the president of United Chemicals. He says that they would be pleased to have Maddy working in their computer department after she has left school – if she wants to, that is. But as a more immediate thank you, he would like to invite you out to Wimbledon tomorrow to the ladies' final, Graf vs. Navratilova, with a treat in their hospitality tent afterwards.»

Maddy und Florian strahlten. Schade, daß Manni nicht mehr hier ist, dachte Florian. *Miss Graf to serve* freute er sich schon auf das Geschehen des nächsten Tages. *Miss Butler to serve* kam ihm sein Traum von der Jacht und der Kurzen wieder in den Sinn. Aber davon erzählte er Maddy lieber nichts. Er nieste.

Wieder läutete das Telefon. Diesmal ging Maddy ran. «Probably Manni or Sakina wanting to know what has happened,» she said.

«No», hörte Florian sie sagen, «nothing at all serious, just a bad cold. It's our weather, you know. He's used to warmer summers. He'll be back on Monday.» She put the phone down.

«That was your language school», she smiled at Florian, «they wanted to know what had happened to you.»

Kriminalgeschichten

Hansjörg Martin
Die Sache mit den Katzen
Ein Krimi, weil es um ein Verbrechen geht, das manche Leute nicht für ein Verbrechen halten
(rotfuchs 344 / ab 10 Jahre)

Klaus Möckel
Bennys Bluff *oder Ein unheimlicher Fall*
(rotfuchs 611 / ab 12 Jahre)
Wie Klaus Möckel, einer der bekanntesten Krimiautoren der ehemaligen DDR, diese verrückt-traurige Geschichte erzählt, «steht haushoch über manchem bemühten Kinderkrimi» (*Frederik Hetmann*).
Kasse Knacken... *Ein Kinderkrimi*
(rotfuchs 673 / ab 11 Jahre)
In seinem neuen Buch erzählt der Autor von der Freundschaft dreier Kinder aus Ost und West, die durch Zufall einer Diebesbande auf die Spur kommen. Das Mädchen Lia gerät in einen schweren Gewissenskonflikt, denn ausgerechnet ihr Bruder scheint mit der Bande zusammenzuarbeiten...

Sylvia Brandis
Español *Rätsel um einen andalusischen Hengst*
(rotfuchs 656 / ab 12 Jahre)
Woher kommt der atemberaubend schöne und kostbare Hengst Español? Weiß der skrupellose Pferdehändler Schimmer mehr als er zugibt? Jan ahnt die Zusammenhänge und weiß von dunklen Geschäften. Eine spannende und brillant geschriebene Abenteuergeschichte um ein Pferd und den schüchternen Jungen Jan Tomsen.

rororo rotfuchs

Emer O'Sullivan / Dietmar Rösler
Butler, Graf & Friends: Umwege
Ein deutsch-englischer Krimi
(rotfuchs 647 / ab 13 Jahre)
Der Fall beginnt am Flughafen, wo Kontrollinstrumente verrückt spielen, und führt zu einer Erpresserbande, die die Arbeit eines genialen Programmierers ausnutzt, der Programme für künstliche Welten erstellt...

Frauke Kühn
« ... trägt Jeans und Tennisschuhe»
(rotfuchs 439 / ab 12 Jahre)
«Ein Kollege meiner Mutter erkannte mich. Ich fand das nicht weiter schlimm. Wer kommt schon auf die Idee, daß der überall herumposaunt, daß man mit mir sehr viel Spaß haben kann..»
Ein Mädchen verschwindet
Krimi
(rotfuchs 519 / ab 14 Jahre)

Kalte Heimat

«Jeder ist ein Ausländer – fast überall.» *(Graffiti)*

Anatol Feid
Achmed M. im Bahnhofsviertel
(rotfuchs 532 / ab 12 Jahre)
Die wahre Geschichte von Achmed M., 12 Jahre, und seinem älteren Bruder, die illegal von Marokko in eine deutsche Großstadt auswandern.

Karlheinz Dürr
Zug nach Danzig *Tomis letzter Ausweg*
(rotfuchs 659 / ab 9 Jahre)

Norbert Ney (Hg.)
Sie haben mich zu einem Ausländer gemacht... *ich bin einer geworden*
(rotfuchs 671 / ab 14 Jahre)
Wie fühlt man sich als Ausländer hier? Müssen wir sie nicht, um Vorurteile zu überwinden, einmal kennenlernen? Ausländer kommen hier selbst zu Wort.

Monika Springer
Fremd wie der Fisch dem Vogel?
Deutsche und türkische Jugendliche fahren in die Türkei. Erzählung
(rotfuchs 578 / ab 13 Jahre)
Deutsche und türkische Schüler brechen zu einer Klassenfahrt in die Türkei auf. Wie sind die Erwartungen, wie reagieren die jungen Deutschen auf das fremde Land, wie die türkischen Jugendlichen auf die Heimat der Eltern? Werden die beiden Gruppen„ miteinander auskommen?

Heinz Knappe
Wolfslämmer *Hava und Jörg dürfen nicht Freunde sein*
(rotfuchs 442 / ab 14 Jahre)

rororo rotfuchs

Dieter Schenk
Der Wind ist des Teufels Niesen
Geschichte eines jungen Zigeuners
(rotfuchs 463 / ab 14 Jahre)
Sarambla und ihre Brüder Merzeli und Stagolo werden wieder einmal aus einem Kaufhaus geworfen. Astrid hat alles beobachtet – und freundet sich mit ihnen an. Sie lernt, daß die Sinti auch heute Angst haben, daß aus dem Wind ein Orkan wird ...-

ky
Heißt du wirklich Hasan Schmidt?
Ein Krimi
(rotfuchs 360 / ab 13 Jahre)
Matthias braucht dringend Geld, aber der Job, der ihm aus der Klemme helfen soll, ist nicht so harmlos. Die Polizei ist hinter ihm her, Türken verstecken ihn. Und auf einmal begreift er, was es bedeutet, wie seine Freundin Shirin und ihre Familie auf der «anderen Seite» zu leben, nicht mehr Matthias, sondern Hasan Schmidt zu heißen ...

Klartext

Geschichten von hier und heute.

Anatol Feid
Im Namen des Volkes *Das Urteil steht noch aus. Jugendliche vor Gericht*
Eine Geschichte
(rotfuchs 541 / ab 14 Jahre)

Irene Rodrian
Blöd, wenn der Typ draufgeht
(rotfuchs 113 / ab 12 Jahre)
Küß mich, Knacki!
(rotfuchs 450 / ab 14 Jahre)

Heidi Hassenmüller
Gute Nacht, Zuckerpüppchen
(rotfuchs 614 / ab 14 Jahre)
Die authentische Geschichte des Mädchens Gaby, das viele Jahre hindurch vom Stief-vater mißbraucht wurde.

Marie-Thérèse Schins
Es geschah an einem Sonntag
Ein Abschied
(rotfuchs 523 / ab 12 Jahre)
Mieke kann Mutter und Vater nicht trösten, sie kann noch nicht einmal sprechen. Ihr ganzer Körper schmerzt. Alles in ihr schreit. Marcel, ihr geliebter Bruder, ist tot...

Ann Ladiges
Mach Druck, Zwiebelfisch!
Eine Gewissensfrage
(rotfuchs 596 / ab 13 Jahre)
Markus, Azubi in einer Druckerei, bewundert den Drucker Georg: der weigert sich aus Gewissensgründen, eine kriegsverherrlichende Heft-Reihe zu drucken und riskiert seinen Job.

Isolde Heyne
Funny Fanny *oder Die Angst vorm Schwarzen Mann*
(rotfuchs 499 / ab 12 Jahre)

rororo rotfuchs

Margret Steenfatt
Nele *Ein Mädchen ist nicht zu gebrauchen*
(rotfuchs 437 / ab 13 Jahre)
«Wenn zwei sich umarmen und küssen, lieben sie sich.» Wolfgang, der Freund ihres Stiefvaters, sucht gezielt die Freundschaft von Nele. Und mißbraucht sie schließlich. Mit einer Adressenliste der Selbsthilfegruppen von Betroffenen.
Haß im Herzen *Im Sog der Gang*
(rotfuchs 648 / ab 12 Jahre)
Tono hält es nicht mehr aus: Kein Platz in der Wohnung, tödliche Langeweile in der Schule... Er sucht Abenteuer in einer Bande, die Angst und Schrecken verbreitet.

Karlhans Frank
Eigentlich habe ich ganz andere Pläne gehabt *Erzählung*
(rotfuchs 502 / ab 14 Jahre)
Anja, Hochleistungssportlerin: keine Zeit für Discos, Jungen oder Eis. Dann hat sie einen Unfall – mit Konsequenzen!

4005/2

Leben in vergangenen Zeiten

Hexen und mutige Frauen, Ritter und Aufständische, Indianer und Piraten – Lebensbilder und aufregende Abenteuer aus vergangenen Zeiten.

Norgard Kohlhagen
Mehr als nur ein Schatten von Glück *Mathilde Franziska Anneke*
Ein Leben in abenteuerlicher Zeit
(rotfuchs 557 / ab 13 Jahre)
«Die Vernunft befiehlt uns, frei zu sein.» 1849 zieht Mathilde Franziska Anneke mit im badisch-pfälzischen Revolutionsheer. Als Soldatin, Journalistin, Frauenrechtlerin und Lehrerin kämpft sie ihr Leben lang für die bürgerlichen Grundrechte.

Willi Bredel
Die Vitalienbrüder *Ein Störtebeker-Roman*
(rotfuchs 24 / ab 11 Jahre)
«Ein freies und fröhliches Leben kennen nur Fürsten, Pfaffen und Piraten», hieß ein Sprichwort im 14. Jahrhundert. Die Vitalienbrüder, Freibeuter in der Nord- und Ostsee, machten den hanseatischen Pfeffersäcken jahrzehntelang die Geschäfte unsicher.

Ulrike Haß
Teufelstanz *Eine Geschichte aus der Zeit der Hexenverfolgung*
(rotfuchs 300 / ab 13 Jahre)
«Marie, meine Liebe, wir müssen jetzt Abschied nehmen.» Ursula Haider wird von den Knechten des Henkers abgeholt – eine Hexe soll sie sein ... Ursula hat wirklich gelebt: in Nördlingen am Ende des 16. Jahrhunderts.

rororo rotfuchs

Heidi Staschen
Verraten, verteufelt, verbrannt
Hexenleben
(rotfuchs 577 / ab 12 Jahre)
Individuelle Lebensgeschichten von Frauen aus der Zeit der Hexenverfolgung

Martin Selber
Faustrecht *Timm Riedbures gefährliche Flucht*
(rotfuchs 93 / ab 9 Jahre)
Nicht einen Tag länger will Timm dem Rittersaß dienen. Nach vielen Abenteuern findet er in Magdeburg Zuflucht. Aber dort herrscht die Pest...

Frederik Hetmann
Der Rote Tag *Bericht über die Schlacht am Litte Bighorn River zwischen den Sioux und Cheyennes und derUS-Kavallerie unter General Armstrong Custer.*
(rotfuchs 275 / ab 13 Jahre)